The pig who wished to be a horse

… and other tales

PETER GILLIES

The pig who wished to be a horse

…and other tales

A·B·C·

abceditions

enjoy life — love others
be you *&* have fun

A·B·C· EDITIONS ◆ FRANCE

The pig who wished to be a horse …and other tales
ISBN 978-2-9546352-6-2

To Almut
my friend

The tales

The pig who wished to be a horse   1

Pope Gelato   11

A picture is worth a thousand words   22

The echo   57

The tale that had no moral   69

The church mouse   87

Death's watch   102

The intractable soul   130

The pig who wished to be a horse

ONCE UPON A TIME, long ago in a kingdom far away, there was a farm that stood at the edge of a small village, nestled in a quiet valley. Above, overlooking the land from a plateau, stood the king's fortress. Escarpments protected the medieval castle's flanks and rear, while a broad grassy slope led down to the valley and the bourg.

In those capricious times, the king of that land was often called upon to defend his kingdom against invading armies. His chosen stallion would be saddled and readied as his cavalry and foot soldiers assembled on the grassy plain, and the king would ride in the vanguard and lead them to battle. On their way, they always travelled by the road that led past the farm. The horses' clattering hooves would send billowing clouds of dust flying as they came near. Through the gateway, the entire army could be seen passing by on its way to war, making such a din and racket that the animals in the farm's central courtyard would yield to panic. The ducks and geese would quack and honk with alarm, the chickens would flap their wings and squawk as they ran in panicked circles, and the farm's many pigs would add their squeals and grunts to the pandemonium.

The king and his army would ride on, the dust would soon settle, and calm would return to the farm. The farmer and his son would go about their chores and pay it no mind. Some time later — the battle fought, the peace secured — the king and his army would pass by the farm once again on their way back to the castle, where a feast would await them. But they were in no hurry, and the horses always walked.

Now, on one such day, as the king was returning from battle on a horse that was not his own and passing by the farm's gate, one of the farmer's fat sows was patiently farrowing a litter of piglets. Two were runts, and these the farmer quickly dispatched. But the others were all prime little swine and were soon put to suckling at their mother's teats. Later, when they were of age to be weaned, they were taken from the sow and transferred to a sty that had been readied for them.

One of these little piglets stood out from all the others. He was strong and husky, sure-footed and bold. The farmer saw that he would grow to be a very fine boar. Every day, the young pig rolled contentedly in the mud and happily ate slops from the trough, greedily pushing past his brothers and sisters with his snout to root in all the corners. You could not help but admire the stiff bristles on his pale pink hide. His tail curled smartly, and he loved to trot briskly about the sty, kicking up his sturdy cloven hoofs with youthful zest.

Life on the farm was very pleasant for the young pig. In the mornings, he would stand at the split-rail fence and watch the goings-on in the courtyard. He was always eager to see if any new chicks would emerge with the hens from the coop, or if the ducks' eggs had hatched. That spring, two calves were born in the barn, and three newborn kids bleated their high-pitched cries above the barnyard din. Oh, the farm was full of new life, including his own, and the pig found everything quite wonderful.

As he grew, though, he discovered there was more to the farm than joyful, new life. One morning, his oldest cousins, fully grown porkers that were kept in the sty closest to the barn, were herded out into the yard by the farmer and his son. There was great excitement among the swine. They grunted and trotted about as the farmer's dogs yapped and nipped at their hocks. The hogs were moved to a holding pen on the far side of the yard. With his head poking past the split rails, the young pig watched as one of his stout, sturdy cousins was led by the farmer and his son to a low-roofed, adjoining outbuilding. The farmer's son opened and then closed the door. For a moment, nothing seemed untoward, but then there was heard an odd, unmistakable sound, a dull thumpy crack, and this was immediately followed by an awful, blood-curdling squeal. The screams that ensued were muffled inside the outbuilding, but the little pig heard them quite distinctly.

That morning, the other farm animals were unusually nervous and quiet as the mysterious cull was repeated time and again. By noon, the holding pen was empty. The young pig had never witnessed this before.

The following day, the farmer and his son thoroughly cleaned the empty sty, filling wheelbarrows with manure and throwing down fresh straw. Then they herded the porkers from the next-closest sty into the one they had prepared. These now counted as the young pig's oldest cousins. Over the course of a week, all of the pigsties were cleaned in turn and the pigs moved one sty down, including the young boar. Soon after, he saw his first sty filled with a new batch of piglets recently farrowed by one of the breeding sows.

So it went, month after month. Now the young pig observed the farm's goings-on with a vague foreboding. He watched as the circle of life began with his father, a ponderous, noisy old boar who grunted and wheezed loudly when put to the task of servicing the sows. Every few weeks, the farmer would lead the boar with a rope out of the barn where he was kept in relative luxury and take him to a stall where a sow was waiting. The old boar knew what to do. He'd sired more offspring over the years than the king's entire army would father in their lifetimes. The farmer kept six breeding sows in all, which he'd bought from other farmers, and bred them in turn. The sows would grow in girth over the course of several months as their gestation ripened. When the piglets were born, the oldest porkers were slaughtered and their meat sold or hung to cure in the farmer's smokehouse. The young boar watched and came to understand what awaited every pig on the farm.

'Poor me!' thought the pig. Often he had watched whenever the king led his army past the farm on their way to defend the kingdom. Oh, how he envied the king's stallion, that handsome steed with his shiny leather saddle, his bridal decorated with colourful guidons. It was thrilling to catch a glimpse of the horse as he cantered past the gate, bearing the king to battle. 'If only I had been born a horse,' lamented the sad pig.

The seasons passed, and every month or so, the pigs were moved to the next sty. The once young piglet was fast approaching his full adult size, and he was indeed a fine boar. The farmer and his son would occasionally stand at the fence and admire him. The pig did not like this attention. He would hear them talking and wonder what they were saying to each other as they looked at him and nodded. Oh, it was better when they picked up their shovels and went back to their chores. At times, there would be much splitting of wood, and fragrant smoke would waft across the yard from the smokehouse chimney day and night for weeks at a stretch. And there were always those terrible days, when the oldest batch of pigs would in their turn disappear through the door of the low-roofed outbuilding, never to be seen again.

Then, one morning, the now adult pig was himself transferred to the very last sty, along with his fellow porkers. Oh, he could stand it no longer. He knew where this was leading. All that day he grunted with despair. And then something even worse occurred. Peering through the fence, he watched as his father was led out of the barn. This time, it wasn't to the sows' stalls that the farmer and his son were taking him. Instead, they led the old boar to the low-roofed outbuilding. However, the two men forgot to close the door, and the pig could see inside. He saw the farmer raise a long-handled sledge above his shoulders, and when he brought it sharply down, there was that dreadful, dull thud. The old boar squealed horribly, gruesomely. For a long while after, his wheezing death cries haunted the air.

By nightfall, the pig was in anguish over his fate. Was death all that awaited him? Was there nothing more, nothing to live for?

'Dear God in Heaven,' prayed the pig. 'Why have You written my fate as a pig? I never wished to be a pig. I do not want to be a pig. Dear Lord, hear my prayer — I wish to be a horse!'

The pig prayed fervently. Over and over, his prayer rose to the heavens, imploring God to make him a horse. Over and over, to be a horse, and not a pig! Until, at last, God grew impatient. Why was no one satisfied with His plan? Why did all of His creatures find fault with their fate? Every day someone, somewhere, would exhort Him, *'O Lord, not this! Spare me!'* They all wanted something else, some other creature's fate. It annoyed Him. Did they think it so very easy, juggling all these criss-crossing causes and intertwined effects? To change one single fate meant numerous adjustments across the board. It was a headache. Too often, it couldn't even be considered. But He always listened to their prayers; and when their petitions were earnest and oft repeated, He generally felt obliged by His position to look into the matter.

The pig was in the midst of reiterating his prayer for an umpteenth time when God's gruff voice broke in on his consciousness.

'What do you want, pig?'

The pig was startled. At first, he was speechless, but then he managed to stammer, 'Is… is that You, God?'

'It's Me. What do you want?'

'O Lord, I want to be a horse,' said the pig, excitedly. 'Please make me a horse!'

This was impossible. The pig could not be a horse. What would the farmer say if he came outside the next morning and found a horse in the pigsty?

But the pig continued.

'I want to be the king's stallion.'

'The stallion?' asked God. 'In the royal stables?'

'Oh, yes, Lord, I want to be the king's horse, the one he rides into battle. I want to be his noble steed. I'm a very fine boar. I'm sure I could be a very fine stallion. The king would be pleased with me. I wouldn't fail him! And it would be better than being a pig.'

This was different. This didn't call for a change of fate or even a miracle, just a small, sleight-of-Hand switch.

'Very well, pig,' answered God. 'When you wake tomorrow morning, you will be the king's horse.'

The pig was overjoyed. He heard God's promise, and he believed. Oh, he was too excited to sleep! But he knew he must. You must fall asleep as a pig if you wish to wake as a horse.

When morning dawned, the pig was woken by the sound of trumpets. Outside there was a great commotion. The pig blinked his eyes. At first, he didn't understand. Where was he? He was standing in a stall, not lying in a muddy sty. Then the doors of the royal stables were thrown open and a dozen stable hands rushed in. They grabbed a handsomely tooled saddle and entered the stall. Oh, God has kept His Word! The pig whinnied with glee. He was saddled, and the stable hands led him outside. The pig saw the king striding towards him from the castle. How thrilling! Could it be? The king was going to ride him! What a strange feeling it was for the pig, when the king swung himself up into the saddle. So that's what it feels like to have a rider on your back! Taking the reins, the king urged his mount forward and the pig gladly broke into a trot. And a very graceful trot, at that. He was, after all, the royal stallion, and the pig discovered in himself an innate sense of how to be a horse. His happiness knew no bounds. Now he was a horse, not a pig destined to be slaughtered!

The king's army was assembling on the great grassy plain. News had come the day before that an enemy prince was invading from the east; a febrile excitement had gripped the castle and preparations were made late into the night. The horses in the stables had been looked after, especially the king's chosen stallion. Now, as the sun's first rays warmed the chill morning air, the king took his place at the head of the vanguard. The trumpets blew, the standards were raised, and the whole company swept down the grassy slope to the road that led past the farm and through the village.

The noisy tumult kicked up by the passing army threw the farmyard animals into the usual panic. The ducks quacked wildly, the geese honked, the chickens ran in circles, and the pigs in the sties all trotted about nervously, grunting and squealing.

There was a mature boar in the last sty, however, who was silent, for he was exceedingly surprised — not to see the king's army passing by, but to find himself in a sty, as a pig. How could it be? Was he not going off to war, to ride with frenzied fear into battle? Oh, joy! What miracle was this? He could hardly contain his relief. He was overwhelmed by a boundless happiness. Why, he was so happy, he even danced a little jig. And very well, too, for now he was a pig!

The king led his army east. By noon, they reached the battlefield where the invading prince had taken up his positions. The trumpeters sounded the charge, and the two armies swept towards each other with mighty shouts and cries. Leading the assault, the king's fine stallion rushed forward like the wind. It was all magnificent and courageous and daring. Sword met sword, with soldiers and horsemen rushing at each other in droves and filling the air with a cacophony of blows and anguished cries as men and horses were slaughtered down the line. The king and the prince found each other in the midst of the fray and fought boldly, swinging their heavy broadswords in great circles. The king's horse acquitted himself bravely in the heat of the battle, but his sidestepping failed to avert the deadly lance that an enemy foot soldier thrust deep into his flank. The fighting raged on. Finally, the king toppled his royal opponent with a mighty, mortal blow, bringing the battle at last to an end.

It was a pitiful sight, that battlefield strewn with the dead and wounded. Men and horses lay everywhere with gaping wounds, their spirits at Death's door. The king's stallion had stood his ground despite the searing pain he felt from the gash in his side, but now, weak and bloodied, he sank to his knees and hocks and collapsed on the grass. The king reached down and stroked his stallion's sad face. 'Thank you, my good horse,' he murmured. 'I wish it had turned out otherwise for you.' Then his attendants brought him another mount, and the king turned to lead his army back home.

The sun was low in the sky that afternoon when the farmer crossed the courtyard. He had nearly finished his chores for the day. Word had earlier reached the village that their king had been victorious in the day's battle. There would be a feast at the castle that night, and good prospects to sell an extra carcass or two. The farmer stepped over the fence into the last sty. He had a rope in his hand, and he looped it round his fine boar's neck.

'Come along, my good fellow. There's a nice piece of work for you to do with the sows.'

He opened the gate and led the pig out. The farmer was very pleased with his new boar.

Pope Gelato

ONCE UPON A TIME, it is said, there was no gelato until it was invented one day by a good, pious man named Pietro.

The good Pietro lived in Christendom's greatest city. Some claim this was Constantinople, but that cannot be, for Pietro lived in Rome, and as the world's Roman Catholics will assure you, the greatest city in all of Christendom is Rome. That is where the Pope, His Eminent Holiness and great Holy Father, resides. He is the Bishop of Rome, the Vicar of Christ, and Good Shepherd to faithful Catholics everywhere.

Now, Pietro was a poor man. He had heard it said that *'The poor shall inherit the Earth'* and he knew this to be true: his father, when he died, had inherited the Earth and was even buried in it. Pietro expected no less for himself in the end. He was good, and he was poor, and he was pious.

One night, God looked down from Heaven into Pietro's good, pious heart. He saw there no ambition, no greed, no covetousness. God was pleased. 'To this son of man,' said God to His angels, 'I will give a blessing.' For blessings and miracles come from Heaven, and only God can bestow them.

The next day, Pietro woke early. The pigeons cooed their morning greetings from the windowsill that overlooked the Piazza Navona, and his lovely wife, Angelina, stirred in her sleep. He patted her rump. Then he got out of bed, dressed in the same clothes he had worn the day before, and went downstairs to eat his breakfast in the back room that served as a kitchen. You can imagine his surprise: on the floor beside the rickety dining table stood a curious machine, the likes of which had never yet been seen nor even imagined. It gleamed with cleanliness. Graceful paddles stood ready in a huge, curved bowl that was cold to the touch. Looking at it, Pietro's sight was clouded by a vision. He saw the paddles churning; he saw sugar and fruits being swept into folds of milk and cream as ice crystals formed; he saw himself filling tubs with the chilled concoction; and he saw scores of eager faces clamouring to buy scoops of the sweet manna dished out in crispy waffle cones.

A single word fell from his lips.

'Gelato.'

This was a gift from God.

With Angelina's help, Pietro soon learned how to work the fantastic machine. Combining fresh milk and cream from nearby dairies with sugar from ships docked in Ostia and fruit from the bountiful Italian countryside, Pietro began concocting myriad sorts of gelato. He opened a tiny shop in the street-side front room, and in no time at all, word of his creation spread throughout Rome. Crowds flocked to the Piazza Navona — they were soon more numerous than the pigeons, and all week long, Pietro would labour, churning out batch after batch.

At first, Pietro and Angelina had refrained from opening their shop on Sundays. That was God's day of rest, after all, a day when all good Catholics must attend to their spiritual duties. But the good people of Rome would come anyway, begging for gelato. Like God, who had toiled six steady days to make the world, so they had toiled all week long, working hard and postponing pleasure. But on the seventh day, God had rested and enjoyed Himself. Didn't they deserve to do the same? Why, when you stopped to think about it, Sundays were the only day a good Christian could truly savour and enjoy a divine scoop of gelato, the only day when — on Earth as it is in Heaven — indolence and delight in worldly perfection might correspond with God on high. Moreover, there were the children to consider. *'Per favore, per i miei bambini,'* they would plead, holding up their hopeful offspring. 'They've been waiting all week. Surely they deserve a treat on Sunday.' And so, although they were pious and good — or perhaps, because they were pious and good — Pietro and Angelina felt called to heed the spirit of the Gospel, wherein Jesus says to His disciples, *'Let the little children come unto me.'*

Now the line to Pietro's shop stretched clear across the Piazza Navona. Torn between earthly rewards and spiritual duties, people who thought they were en route to Saint Peter's would find themselves veering off course to join the queue for a cone. 'I was good this week,' they would rationalise. 'God knows my heart is pure. Surely He's not expecting me to go to Mass every

Sunday.' The bells would toll the Church's call to prayer, but their unwilling soles would fail to carry the faithful across the Tevere in time to cross themselves.

So it was that one Sunday, the Pope, entering Saint Peter's to say Mass as was his custom, was surprised to find the vast nave half-empty of worshippers. Indeed, several choir singers were absent as well. 'What is the cause of this?' he whispered to Cardinal Thomas, who sat beside him. The cardinal shrugged his shoulders and pursed his lips with smug disapproval.

'They're no doubt playing truant. You know how they are, like naughty little children.'

Returning to his apartments afterwards, the Pope called for his physician.

'Is there an epidemic in the city?' he asked. 'Are the good citizens of Rome sick at home with the flu? Are they bedridden with plague?'

'Why, no, your Holiness. So far as I know, there have been no pandemics of late,' replied the doctor.

The following week, the Pope discovered that his congregation had dwindled still further. The choir was reduced to one baritone and four aging sopranos whose quavering tremolos made the Pope feel squeamish. He said the Mass, but when all was said and done, he was astonished to see half the remaining worshippers jumping from their seats and rushing to the doors.

Come the next Sunday, though, the Pope could hardly believe his eyes. The great basilica was practically empty. The choir stalls were deserted, the organist nowhere to be seen, and there wasn't even an usher on hand to collect the weekly tithe. 'And where on earth is Cardinal Thomas? He was supposed to read the homily.' The Pope, Blessed Head of the One True Church, was left to celebrate the Mass for a meagre gathering of sour-faced biddies and apathetic geezers, a dessert-hating congregation of downturned mouths who mumbled the Mass with rote conviction and geriatric indifference.

'By God, the Holy Church cannot go on like this,' fumed the Pope afterwards in the vestiary. Donning his ordinary robes, he left the Vatican and crossed the Tevere in search of answers. The streets of Rome were nearly as silent and empty as his church, but he soon heard laughter. Following it to the Piazza Navona, the Pope was astounded to find the great square overflowing. Everywhere he looked, he saw smiling, happy faces. A seemingly endless, serpentine line zigzagged across the piazza and led the Pope's gaze to a single door, out of which emerged at that very moment Cardinal Thomas, His Eminence's fat pink tongue passionately caressing a triple scoop cone of gelato.

Furious — and ignoring the angry young woman who hollered after him, *'Hey, no cutting in line! Who do you think you are, the Pope?'* — the irate Holy Father marched across the piazza and pushed his way in through the door.

'Whose shop is this?' the Pope demanded to know.

Angelina immediately recognised the man who stood before the counter.

'Oh, your Holiness, please forgive me,' she blurted fearfully, curtsying and bowing at the same time.

'No forgiveness until you tell me who owns this shop,' snapped the pious P. P.

'My husband, Your Holiness. My husband, Pietro.'

'Where is he? I will see him at once.'

Angelina nearly collapsed with dread and shame as she directed the Pope through the low doorway that led to the back room.

'What is the meaning of this?' barked the Pope, bursting in upon Pietro. The poor man was so startled that he nearly toppled over into a tub of stracciatella. The Pope was unmoved. 'What are you doing?' he pursued. 'Why are you tempting good Christians away from Mass and their spiritual duties?'

God in Heaven, attentively watching all this from above, decided that divine intervention was in order. Stilling His good servant's pounding heart and muting his clumsy tongue, God guided Pietro's hand as it scooped up a glistening sphere of red raspberry gelato and offered it in a cone to the Pope.

Without a word, the Pope took the proffered cone and looked at it suspiciously. Then he licked the surface of the creamy nectar. In an instant, he understood the danger. This was Satan's doing!

'We will see about this,' vowed the Vicar of Christ, turning on his heel. He stormed out of the room and brushed past Angelina.

'Oh, Your Worship,' she begged, 'Please say you'll forgive us!'

But the Pope was already out the door. He made a beeline for the Vatican, stopping only once as he crossed the bridge to throw the offending gelato into the Tevere. Regaining his apartments, he called for his secretary.

'Convene the Sacred Curia,' he ordered.

The very next day, a papal bull was issued, and the edict was immediately delivered to Pietro at his shop. In sum, it announced that the eating of gelato on Sundays would be strictly forbidden, and that all shops must be closed for business as well. The Pope added, in a handwritten addendum, 'I'll expect to see you at Mass!' The bull was tacked to Pietro's shop door, and all week long an unabated gathering of onlookers read and reread the decree, shaking their heads and murmuring in hushed tones.

The following Sunday, a stream of churchgoers mournfully crossed the Tevere to attend Mass at Saint Peter's. They were sullen and silent, and they cast sideway glances at Pietro and Angelina, who looked at their shoes and felt as if God's Wrath were scorching their immortal souls. When the Pope strode into the basilica, he looked with satisfaction at the overflowing nave. 'A full house! This is how things should be every Sunday,' he chortled. That is, until he looked closer. A sea of glum faces stared at him from every row. Even his old friend, Cardinal Thomas, looked dejected in his straight-backed ecclesiastical chair. The organist opened the service with a few lugubrious bars from a requiem before segueing to the first hymn, but the choir did not follow suit; dispirited, ignoring their cue, they opted instead for the sorrowful words of the dirge.

Standing at the altar, the Pope found himself struggling through the Mass. He had never felt so solitary. As he conferred the consecrated Host on each penitent tongue kneeling before him at the rail, he could not escape the uneasy sense that he was administering the last rites to the entire body of Christ. Finally, bringing the ordeal to an end with the words *Ite, missa est,* he closed his missal with relief and swept hastily from the chancel.

That week, all of Rome sank into depression. The citizens, ordinarily happy and carefree, grew careworn and miserable. By Friday, the pervasive melancholia so alarmed the town authorities that they hurried to the Vatican and begged for an audience.

'Holy Father,' they pleaded, 'you must reconsider. We do humbly beseech you: rescind your decree. If you refuse to yield, it will surely lead to the downfall of Rome. The people love God and will gladly worship Him — but they cannot live without gelato!'

Although the Pope had thought himself inured to doubt, he could not forget the overwhelming sense of doom that had besieged the basilica Sunday last. Gravely, he assured the townsmen he would consider their petition. Then he retired to his chambers. 'See that I am not disturbed,' he instructed his secretary. Undertaking a lonely vigil, the Pope pondered the question throughout the night. He sought solace in meditation, guidance in the Gospels. *'Verily I say unto you,'* he read, *'to enter the Kingdom of Heaven, you must become as children.'* He scrutinized the Last Supper and mulled the many facets of the Church's rites of Holy Communion. He even prayed a few times, fervently, until he could endure it no longer. Finally, he collapsed on his bed and slept.

God looked down from Heaven and shook His Head. 'What do you do with such a man?' He muttered. The angels shrugged their wings and flew in insouciant circles. Heaving a Sigh, God took pity and kindled an illumination. The Pope woke with the sun's first rays pouring through the window. They melted the sleep from his eyes, and when he opened them, he suddenly knew what he must do.

Stealing out of the Vatican, the Pope rushed to the Piazza Navona. All was deserted at that early hour. He knocked at the shop's door. While he waited for someone to open, he removed the papal bull that was posted there and tore it in half.

'Oh, Your Holyship,' stammered Pietro when he opened the door.

'Holiness,' corrected the Pope, hastily concealing the torn bull beneath his robes and slipping inside.

That afternoon, passersby in the Piazza Navona gathered before Pietro's shop to read a new papal bull posted on the door. Word spread across the city like wildfire.

'COME TO SAINT PETER'S FOR MASS,' read the decree. 'GOD'S FORGIVENESS AND GELATO FOR ALL!'

The basilica was already thronged with eager penitents when the bells began pealing the next day, and the nave could hardly contain the crowd. Before a sea of expectant, hopeful faces, the Pope, intoning the liturgy's holy words, consecrated quantities of crisp waffle cones and buckets of raspberry gelato, transmuting them into the veritable body and blood of Christ. Then, with the good, pious Pietro on hand to assist him, the Pope stood at the railing and doled out individual servings of the consecrated Eucharist to each and every one of the faithful.

From then on, Rome's joyous Catholics would flock to Saint Peter's. Pope Gelato, as he came to be affectionately known, would greet his parishioners on the steps. Every Mass ended with a delicious Eucharistic offering: the cone, the consecrated waffle-wafer body of Christendom's Blessed Saviour, the gelato, the gelid symbol of His freely offered blood sacrifice, so delectable it would melt the hardest of hearts. Flavours varied throughout the year. In turn there would be red cherry, watermelon, strawberry, raspberry, pomegranate, and even, on the holiest feast days, pink grapefruit. For Easter, Pietro would churn out batches made with blood oranges.

All this went on for a long, happy time. The good Pope's masses became the talk of Rome, and the Catholic Church grew in prestige around the world. Ever good and pious, Pietro never tired of making gelato, and because the Church manoeuvred to be his sole client and dictated the terms of their contract by papal bull, he was guaranteed to remain poor as well. Looking down from Heaven upon all this as it played out, God shrugged.

But nothing lasts forever. One day, time ran out on the good Bishop of Rome and he went to join that great Papa in the Sky. The bells of Saint Peter's tolled night and day, mourning the Church's sad loss. The Sacred College was convened to elect a new Pope. But the cardinals were divided. Some were jealous and resentful of the *defunctus* Pope's popularity, and they sat with downturned mouths and raised their voices for change. The votes dragged on inconclusively. Black smoke poured and poured from the Vatican chimney week after week, until at last, a tentative white puff wafted upwards. Soon after, the newly elected Pope appeared and, from the pulpit of Saint Peter's central balcony, announced to the expectant crowd that he was cut from a different cloth than his predecessor.

And he was! Paragon of the Dark Ages, the old sourpuss was a wizened old geezer with a downturned mouth who couldn't even bear to look at gelato. 'Satan's doing!' declared the new Pope in his first papal bull, issued to annul the Church's Eucharistic contract. On pain of excommunication, Pietro and Angelina were forbidden to mix milk, cream and sugar in any way, shape or form, and Catholics everywhere were banned from ever again savouring the divine gift of gelato within the confines of God's Holy Church.

Which is why, even to this day throughout Italy, one sees pictograms such as this posted at the entry to every Catholic Church.

A picture is worth a thousand words

T HEY'D BEEN BICKERING for weeks, those two.

Francis de Sales, patron saint of writers, had been lording it over no less a person than Luke the Apostle, patron saint of artists. Words had finally gained the upper hand.

From the dawn of Eden, Luke had been resting easy on his laurels. Every year it was the same: when it came time for God to review His saints and award them kudos and rank them all in a carefully assayed pecking order of saintly merit, Luke had always stood head and shoulders above the likes of Francis. No wonder: pictures had been mankind's penchant since its first bipedal days. Progress had been slow but steady over the millennia, until Neanderthal man and his sapient contemporaries had evolved into image-makers, par excellence. Words? They hadn't gotten past the stage of guttural spiels and long-winded humping. Writing? Man could hardly drag a stick in a straight line, much less delineate an alphabet. But as God's creation spun incessantly through its diurnal circles and yearly orbits, civilisation could only advance in leaps and bounds. Man was soon scaling the heights of linguistic complexity and upping the ante. More than ever, he wanted to write. Divining the danger, Luke goaded the Sumerians with reeds, browbeating them to invent cuneiform, and persuaded the Most High that its pictographs counted for pictures. They became all the rage. The apostle was lulled into believing things would always be so easy. But Francis didn't fancy being an underdog-saint all his life. Working tirelessly to advance his cause, he abetted the Ugarits in stealing off with Akkadian cuneiform; shorn of its ideographic links and simplified, it spawned the first alphabet. Luke cried foul and copyright infringement. So Francis turned to the Phoenicians living in Byblos and pressed them to chisel out an entirely new system loosely derived from some proto-Sinaitic scratchings that had escaped Luke's notice when he'd been busy teaching hieroglyphs to the Egyptians. It was a start that soon paid handsome dividends. Luke fought back. He signed the Chinese to an exclusive use of logograms and took pictographs to the Mayas. Redoubling his efforts, Francis wisely decided to let his writing system evolve willy-nilly; in no time at all, myriad new alphabets sprang up worldwide.

Until it finally happened. One All Saints Day, seated before the whole congregation convened in the Great Heavenly Hall for the annual festivities, God called out Francis' name before Luke's.

Luke's mouth dropped.

'What?' he blurted. 'You can't be serious!' His challenge rebounded off the celestial dome.

But God was serious. Sorely irritated by His saint's ill-mannered temerity, the Almighty interrupted Himself to take

His saint to task.

'Look here, Luke,' He snapped. 'Are you doubting our accounting? The numbers don't lie. In the past year, it's quite clear: more words were written than pictures drawn.'

'But they were written with my pictographs!' protested Luke — adding hopefully, 'Weren't they?'

'Balderdash,' thundered God. 'The alphabets have taken the lead. I've got angels in every corner, watching developments from every angle.'

It was news to Luke. Oh, he was livid! He nearly blew a fuse right there in the ranks. How it galled him to see that smug Francis swishing his robes, practically walking on air as he swept up to take his place in line. Alphabets! Just a jumbled bunch of squiggly loopings and lines. A page full of text was an eyesore.

The ceremony resumed with pomp and circumstance. When God finally called his name, Luke found out how far down he'd slid: he now ranked on a par with Saint Gangulphus, patron saint of tanners, and Saint Hubertus, patron saint of hunters and furriers. The humiliation was nearly as hard to bear as the odours wafting from the robes of the two saints with whom he had to stand shoulder to shoulder for the group bow.

The buffet afterwards, badly catered, did nothing to mollify Luke's rage. The highest-ranking saints gathered round Francis; he was fêted and praised, and they offered him cigars and champagne and caviar canapés as they drew him into their clique. Luke had been a regular fixture in that coterie since time immemorial. Now he was suddenly downgraded to soft drinks and chips, rubbing elbows with the likes of Saint Malo and Thérèse de Lisieux.

'Don't let it get you down,' said Saint Matthew, coming up to put a friendly hand on his fellow apostle's shoulder. 'Look at me: patron saint of accountants and tax collectors, bankers and bookkeepers. Compared to barter these days, I'm sitting on nothing but a small-time numbers racket. You think that's going to change any time soon?'

Luke had never much cared for Matthew. What kind of brains did it take to reign over ten lousy digits? The guy wasn't exactly a simpleton, but he wasn't much fun at a party, either. His tales of intercession mostly amounted to changing zeros into nines — or threes into eights, or ones into sevens — and his stories always sounded wonky from the start. He attracted the weirdest kinds of people.

Just then, a glum looking Saint Dominic shuffled by none too steadily, clutching a watery Shirley Temple.

'What's with him?' Luke wondered aloud.

Matthew stifled a nascent guffaw.

'You didn't hear about Domi? He found out the universe is expanding.'

Luke turned to Matthew with a blank expression.

'So?'

'What do you mean, so? The dummy thought God was done making the Creation. That he'd never have more than a few trillion stars to juggle with, at most. Only he just found out that God is expanding the universe even faster than the speed of light, springing new stars out of nowhere by the gazillion.'

Dominic had sat down wearily in an armchair over by the big bay windows. He'd drained his glass and was staring into space, forlornly chewing a maraschino cherry.

'And *so*?' insisted Luke testily, crunching on an ice cube.

'Well, since Domi's the patron saint of stargazers, God wants him to catalogue and track every single new star that comes up in the sky — giant, dwarf, nova, you name it. He even threw in the black holes. Can you beat that? Domi says it just goes to show the Big Guy's addled. "Why should I track black holes?" he says. "No one's ever gonna see them."'

Matthew shook his head. When you stopped to think about Who you were working for, you couldn't help but wonder whether sainthood was all it was cracked up to be.

'Can you imagine, Luke? Dealing with all those stars, one by one? Not being able to reduce them to an exponential shorthand and be done with it? Lemme tell you, I sure wouldn't want to be in Domi's robes.'

Luke didn't understand what Matthew was talking about, but he reasoned that Matthew didn't either. The fellow's head was befuddled with numbers.

'See, that's what I like about digits,' confided Matthew. 'Even for a big job, you only need a few. Heck, with just two or three, you can talk about things in the thousands, hundreds of thousands. Even billions, if you want.'

Luke swigged the last of his fizzled bitter lemon and set down the glass. He wondered how many screws were loose in Matthew's head. Truly, it was a miracle that accountants relied on the guy.

'Wait a minute,' he gasped, gripping Matthew's arm. 'What did you just say? About only needing a few? What do you mean?'

Startled by Luke's sudden ardour, Matthew looked at his sleeve. Had his fellow apostle been eating the chips? He didn't want greasy spots on his ceremonial robes.

'Just that,' he answered, gently prying Luke's fingers from his arm. 'Sometimes you can reduce a huge number to a simple, exponential expression.'

'Like what?' panted Luke excitedly.

'Well, let me think,' murmured Matthew. He stroked his unkempt beard for thought. 'For example, you can write 9,509,900,499 as 99^5 — see, it only takes three little digits to indicate an arithmetical value of over nine and a half billion. If Domi could do that with his stars, he'd be on easy street.'

'That's it,' cried Luke, smacking his palm with his fist. 'You're a godsend, Matthew.' Beside himself with joy, Luke dashed off. 'I owe you one!'

Matthew looked at his sleeve and sighed. He wouldn't be forgetting his conversation with Luke any time soon.

☙

Determined to unseat Francis, Luke requested an audience with God.

'A matter of utmost importance,' he explained to the domination in charge of the Supreme Being's Holy Book of

Appointments.

Luke watched the celestial secretary flip lazily through a dozen blank pages. She paused now and then, pursed her angel lips once or twice, and finally sighed with resignation.

'I can squeeze you in two weeks from today,' she offered.

'Two weeks? Surely you have something sooner,' pleaded Luke.

'I'm sorry. From where I sit, He's all booked up. It's the best I can do. Ten o'clock?'

Luke hadn't seen a single engagement pencilled in, but even so, he knew he was in no position to argue. Angels outranked saints, on account of their wings. God liked them because they were useful for fanning His Brow when he sat on His throne. As He was fond of pointing out, *Angels make wind. Saints break wind.*

'Very well,' said Luke. 'In two weeks, then. That's Luke, Apostle. L-U-K-E. Aren't you going to write it down?'

'No need. I'll remember,' purred the domination with an insincere, beatific smile. 'See you then. Have a nice day.'

⅓

For a fortnight, Luke had to put up with Francis' newfound glory. Whenever they bumped into each other in the celestial hallways, Francis would make a point of appearing busy.

'Can't stop to chat,' he would say. 'You remember how it was, don't you, when you had so many people praying to you night and day.'

Observing how often errors crept into written texts down on Earth, Luke let drop that Francis should perhaps intercede more often for spellchecking on behalf of his followers. 'And can't you get them to abide by a few simple rules of grammar?' he needled further. 'Or even punctuation?' But Francis didn't want to encumber his people with exactitude, lest they wane in their enthusiasm for the written word. And he was leery of things like commas and quotes, fearful they might be counted as ornamental flourishes and credited to Luke's tally; until his position as leader was secure, he preferred to leave punctuation by the wayside. Meanwhile, he was quick to counter that Luke's legions of artists were still clumsy when it came to perspective and proportions.

'Say, Luke, when are you going to enlighten them about vanishing points?' he chided one day in passing. 'Euclid may as well have never lived, for all the use your artists make of perspective. And I've noticed your followers sure have some amateurish notions with regard to human anatomy. God made man in His Image, but to look at the primitive artefacts your brood is turning out, no one would ever know it.'

The Apostle simmered and steamed, but kept his cool as Francis floated on down the hall, loftily claiming he had urgent business in Seventh Heaven on Cloud Nine.

'Just you wait, you old gloat,' muttered Luke under his breath, clenching his fists in the sleeves of his robes.

Meanwhile, he prepared his coup. He saw to borrowing a few dozen fine pictures from his friends the Egyptians, and he went looking for a loquacious ally, someone he could call on to offer a discourse that would be judicially accepted as impartial. He soon settled on 'golden-mouthed' John. The voluble patron saint of orators was linked in the minds of the heavenly host to words, not pictures; no one would charge John Chrysostom with having a personal interest in promoting art over writing. Nor did Luke have reason to fear the spoken word; speech was tallied as music to the ears, and so never counted in Francis' favour.

At last, the big day came. The apostle arrived at ten o'clock sharp with John in tow and quite a few strong-armed virtues who had been sent by the domination to help with the exhibits. Hovering to greet them, the angelic secretary winningly flashed her carefully practiced beatific smile.

'Good morning, good morning! The Lord will be with you all shortly. Won't you make yourselves comfortable here in the lounge? And please, do feel free to enjoy some of our complimentary refreshments.'

Crowding through the door to the waiting room, the virtues dropped the pictures and flew to the doughnuts while John, close on their heels, strategically chose a chair situated next to a tray heaped with golden French pastries. Trailing in behind, Luke considered the crullers, but found he was too nervous to stomach the idea of food. He sank into a chair and watched with veiled queasiness as his fellow saint scarfed three croissants in quick succession, washing them down with black coffee. *Your robes,* despaired the apostle. *Don't soil your robes.* But John slurped and feasted freely; several java droplets fell right down his front, and his freshly pressed robes were soon speckled with a lapful of buttery flakes. Meanwhile, the angelic virtues were busily stuffing their cherubic mouths with doughnut holes and chattering gaily.

The domination soon returned and with a melodious lilt announced, 'The Lord will receive you now.'

Preceding the others, who were hastily licking their sugar-coated fingers and brushing crumbs from their robes, Luke followed the angel. She ushered him into the imposing celestial chambers. God was waiting for them. His mighty throne was set on a dais and encircled by a score of seraphim at His beck and call, who were softly chanting the Trisagion and seated in stiff-backed chairs.

Luke bowed low, as dictated by protocol.

'My Lord and God,' he professed, 'Your humble servant Luke the Apostle doth greet You. Praise be unto the Lord.'

God minced no words.

'Cut to the chase, Luke. What's on your mind?'

Straightening up and turning briefly to see if John and the virtues were behind him, Luke was staggered to discover Francis de Sales standing by the wall.

'What are you doing here?' he exclaimed with surprise.

'That was My idea,' interposed God bluntly. 'Let's get on with it, shall We?'

His rival's unexpected presence quite unsettled Luke. Obviously, God had divined his intent. He'd have to play his hand closely.

'Yes, Lord, yes, just as soon as John and the others join us. Ah, here they are now. Come right in. Please, won't you set the paintings along the wall there? Excuse me, Francis—I'm sorry, could you move yourself over here to make room? Thank you so much.' Eying the virtues' sticky fingers, Luke added quickly, 'I think John and I can manage things from here on, boys. Don't you, John? Why don't you fellows take the rest of the morning off? Go get yourselves some more doughnuts.'

God was drumming His Fingers on the arm of His throne and gnashing His Teeth as the domination herded the giggling virtues out the door and closed it behind her.

'There, I think we're ready now,' said Luke merrily.

'I'm waiting,' growled God. With a brusque wave of His Hand, He silenced the chanting seraphim.

Luke paused, then turned with purpose. Drawing himself up, he addressed the august assembly with aplomb.

'Lord! I have come to ask that You reconsider the worth of a word compared to an image. No one was happier than I to see Francis rise among the ranks of saints on behalf of his alphabet-wielding wordsmiths, but I believe You do an injustice to artists everywhere when You value pictures on a par with words. The one-to-one ratio You have set sorely belittles the merits of art, and grossly underrates the unceasing toil that artists must furnish to realise their sublime creations. Have You considered where all this might lead, should artists learn their best works count for no more than a trifling word? Do You wish for mankind to abandon visual beauty altogether?'

Francis arched his brows deprecatingly.

'What do you propose?' sighed God, perceiving the apostle's guile but bound to hear him out.

'Well, Lord — and may I add that I'm delighted Francis has joined us this morning,' interjected Luke, 'because I think he might benefit from taking a more humble view of all those words his alphabets spawn — I'd like to suggest that we ask an impartial observer, such as John Chrysostom here, patron saint of the spoken *word*, to describe a simple picture. I invite You, Lord, to pick just one from among these many examples I've brought. Let us hear for ourselves how many words John needs, to give a fair description of an image that was gauged by Your angels as being equal to but one single word written by Francis' scribblers.'

A hushed murmur broke out in the bevy of angels seated round the throne.

'Stop twittering,' huffed God. 'Go procure parchment and quills. We will make a record of the proceedings.'

The seraphim flew from their seats and sped off to the celestial storeroom for supplies.

'Very well, Luke,' He agreed. 'I'm willing to consider the matter. John?'

'Yes, Lord?' Realising with baffled dismay that he'd forgotten to genuflect when he first came in, the saint hastened to bow reverently and was mortified to discover the coffee stains on his robes. Just then, the angels returned to the chamber with a noisy flurry of beating wings. John took advantage of the commotion to quickly turn his robes round back to front.

God was glaring at the angels, wishing they'd hurry up and settle down. When at last calm descended, God turned His attention back to the saint.

'See that picture there, John?' He resumed, pointing to the very smallest image Luke had brought.

'I see it, Lord,' answered John, still kneeling.

'Without undue strain or effort, I want you to describe it for Us,' commanded God.

John Chrysostom rose to the task. With all the passion and fervour you'd expect from the patron saint of orators, he launched into a description of the picture in the minutest of detail, bringing to life its myriad shades of colour and texture, its suggestive narrative, its historical context, its iconography and compositional elements. Luke couldn't have picked a better advocate for his cause. Francis de Sales was aghast. True to form, the windy saint went on and on, and even the seraphim — no strangers to ceaseless chanting — were awed. 'Golden-mouthed' John spoke eloquently and without pause for over six and a half hours. In their collective record of his testimony, the recording angels churned out more than four hundred parchment pages — though their quills were so dulled by the exercise that no one could later decipher what they had written. In answer to God's query, the chief seraphic stenographer roughly calculated that John had spoken no less than 100,000 words to describe the picture, 'give or take a thousand.'

Though footsore from standing throughout the ordeal, Luke was delighted.

'You see, Lord?' he crowed with manifest satisfaction. 'Not just *one* word was needed, but *one hundred thousand!*'

'So I heard,' groaned God.

'But Lord,' objected Francis, 'this is blatant exaggeration!

Not every picture or drawing needs so many words to describe it. Why, some can be handily summed up in just a few, like *stick figure man* or *crow's foot mark*. Would Luke have us believe that every ink-scratch his artists dash off is worth one hundred thousand words? It's an outrage!'

Luke conceded the point, but played up the fact that even Francis had needed three words to describe the simplest of figures. 'My Lord, a single word is wonderful, there is no doubt; but an image created by man is indubitably worth more. Clearly, the one-to-one ratio your angels are using to tally the merits of writers versus artists is specious.'

Though He hated having to admit as much to the apostle, God had to agree.

'We will adjourn for a one hour recess,' He decided, playing for time.

With rustling robes and beating wings, saints and seraphim dutifully withdrew. Furrowing His Brow, God convened the archangels who were responsible for conducting the annual census of saintly merits. Together, they debated the issue: how many words should a picture be worth? God's foremost criterion was that whatever they decided, the rule should have a nice ring to it. He hadn't gotten to where He was by neglecting poetry, and You weren't going to win kudos by announcing that a picture was worth, say, seventy-five-thousand-six-hundred-and-twelve words. But God also wanted a figure that would keep Luke in check. He didn't want His apostle getting cocky. Wrestling with the conundrum, the heavenly host tried out dozens of ratios and presented the various outcomes.

Some put Luke so far ahead of Francis that artists, prone as they were by their very nature to an exaggerated sense of self-importance, would likely lose touch with reality *en masse* and decide that their creations put them not only on a pedestal above their fellow man, but on a par with God Himself; while others so trivialized the importance of artists' divinely inspired works that God was afraid Luke's arty protégés, who were no less prone to taking offence, might yield to the siren song of despair *en bloc* and wipe themselves out in one fell swoop with a collective suicide.

Meanwhile, the three saints and the seraphim were cooling their heels in the lounge. Luke, now famished, had been disappointed to discover that the virtues had greedily devoured the rest of the doughnuts, crullers and all. He was just about to lay claim to the last remaining croissant when John blithely picked it up and took a large bite, chasing it with coffee and spilling more dribbles down his robe, this time on the back, which he was wearing to the front. It looked as though he'd been out bicycling on a wet, muddy street. Luke winced and resigned himself to hunger pangs. For their part, the seraphim had polished off the spongy cucumber sandwiches and were now batting balled-up napkins round the room, using two trash cans for baskets and making quite a ruckus as they flew about, bouncing off the walls. The domination looked in at one point, but the seraphim outranked her and she thought better of rebuking them.

Feeling quite pleased with the performance he'd pulled off in the celestial chambers, John came up to Luke and held forth about the merits of formal orations read from prepared notes, compared to extemporaneous speeches. Brushing dandruff-like flakes of pastry from his fellow saint's sleeves, Luke nonchalantly disagreed. He urged John to inspire his followers to do more off-the-cuff work.

'I think written texts make for tedious lectures and ho-hum sermons,' he slyly opined. 'What's the good of actually writing out a speech beforehand? It shoots down flights of fancy and smothers impromptu insights.'

As for Francis de Sales, he was sitting by himself, keeping his own counsel. How he rued crying victory too soon. Luke's clever complaint had indeed turned the tables; there could be no doubt that words were going to be devalued and pictures reappraised. The only question was by how much. God hadn't looked too happy with Saint John's long-winded palavering. Saint Brevity he was not. Perhaps Luke would lose points for that. Still, there was quite a lot of ground between three and one hundred thousand. Would God split the difference and round up? Would a picture be worth 49,999 words? Francis shuddered at the idea.

A small bell sounded. The proceedings were reconvened.

❧

'Very well, Luke. We've considered your gripe, and We agree: a picture is worth more than a word. Accordingly, the ratio used for calculating your and Francis' relative merits each year is to be revised,' announced God.

Luke was beaming. A fleeting vision of caviar clouded his mind's eye.

'However, that said, We impose two provisos.'

God fixed Luke with His holy Gaze. Assuming a more deferential posture, the apostle adjusted his smile, aiming for a cross between beatific and ingenuous.

'First: art must never sink to being just a sketchy affair. As Francis has correctly pointed out, some drawings truly amount to very little. We must have a full range. If your artists are found to be dashing off nothing but doodles with an eye to boosting your numbers, We'll soon hear of it, and you'll know My Wrath.'

God now turned to Francis and John.

'Second: verbosity must be curbed. There is nothing more wasteful of time and patience than the prolix use of words. The rule is, *Long enough to cover the subject, short enough to be interesting.* Angels will be looking for unforgivable instances of tautology, pleonasm, and periphrasis. Clear violations will be docked from your scores.'

John Chrysostom shrank somewhat, sure that God was singling him out. He suddenly regretted having let Luke talk him into coming. He also felt very self-conscious about his robes, which he'd turned sideways to no good effect.

'What about reiteration?' piped up Luke, hoping to tighten the screws on his rival.

God frowned.

'Reiteration, though annoying except in small doses, is a necessary rhetorical evil. I won't qualify it as a sin.'

'How about misspellings?' tried the apostle.

'Forbidden. I will not condone gibberish. Misspelled words will be struck from the record.'

That brought a smile to Luke's face. Francis decided to bite the bullet. He may as well know where he stood.

'What about punctuation, Lord, or accent marks? How will those be tallied?'

God felt compassion for Francis, who wasn't at the end of his troubles. He decided to do him a good turn.

'Diacritics are more than just decorative,' He ruled. 'They are specific to pronunciation, and therefore to words. Consequently, accents may be used freely in any writing system, with no credit accruing to Luke. As for punctuation, its myriad marks were introduced to aid John's flock in the oral delivery of written texts. But as they likewise serve to disambiguate, and to clarify syntax, each mark will be counted in your favour for as many words as it takes to call them to mind.'

'So a comma or colon will count for one word each?' asked Francis, brightening.

'One word each,' confirmed God. 'The same goes for dash, parenthesis, ellipsis, apostrophe, semicolon, and so forth. Although their only role is to maintain order, when appearing in text they will be tallied on your behalf as words.'

It was a small but meaningful victory for Francis.

'But surely exclamation mark or quotation mark won't be counted as two?' protested Luke. The idea of Francis getting all that cushy credit for punctuational glyphs unnerved him.

God narrowed His Eyes till they were snake-like slits.

'Yes, Luke, they will count for two,' He ruled — 'as will full stop.' There was a steely edge to His Voice. The God of Heaven was in no mood to brook dissent.

Luke checked himself. At this rate, the next thing you knew, God would be divesting him of his Egyptian hieroglyphs and Chinese logograms, claiming that writers everywhere, no matter what system they used, were only putting words down on paper. The apostle bit his tongue, hoping to forestall any further erosion to his shrinking sphere of influence.

'No other questions, then?' asked the Most High. 'Or objections?' He added, for Luke's benefit.

The saints shook their heads.

'Good. Then I will spell it out for you.'

Raising His Voice so that it would boom throughout Heaven, God rose from His throne and proclaimed:

'A PICTURE IS WORTH A THOUSAND WORDS!'

❧

Luke was hopping mad.

'A measly thousand words!' he complained to Catherine of Bologna, a sympathetic ear. 'Can you beat that? It hardly makes picking up a brush worthwhile at all. Why should anyone learn to draw?'

It hadn't mattered in the least to Luke that his latest ranking had been recalculated according to the new rate, leading to his being duly reinstated among the first tier of saints. What rankled was having to keep his shoulder to the wheel. Had

God valued pictures at ten-thousand-to-one, he would have left Francis far behind. Fifty-thousand-to-one would have put him head and shoulders above even Saint George, who had recently squeaked past Peter the Apostle to be named Saint of the Year. And though he'd hardly dared hope for more, it had crossed his mind that a rate of one-hundred-thousand-to-one would have so increased his stature that he could have aspired to being made Patron Saint of Saints.

But at a thousand-to-one, Luke had no choice. Just to maintain his standing, he'd have to work like the dickens. Francis wasn't going to fade away, and God's gift of punctuation would only embolden him. The race was on.

∾

For a long while, it was touch and go for Luke. In the hotly contested Middle Eastern theatre, Francis' alphabets spread in every direction, inexorably superseding Luke's precious pictograms. Learned men began writing treatises on every topic imaginable. If you could talk about it, you could write about it, and the feat was so impressive that authors came to be revered. In Europe, their manuscripts were reproduced by armies of scribes calligraphing night and day, and every single word counted in Francis' favour. To meet the challenge, Luke courted Rome. Persuading popes that treasure on Earth was akin to treasure in Heaven, the apostle saw to it that churches and cathedrals throughout Christendom were decorated floor to ceiling with paintings and frescos and mosaics. The preparatory work produced legions upon legions of drawings, and Luke ensured that no sketch, no study, no draft or plan went uncounted. He even wormed his way into Francis' fief, securing work for his artists to illuminate manuscripts and supply illustrations.

Taking the bull by the horns, Francis cleverly converted the Muslims to an abhorrence of pictorial representation, but Luke petitioned God to give him half-credit for ornate decorative work based on words. Although he could not prevent North Africa from falling to Arabic, the apostle stirred up sandstorms and saw to it that the contagion did not easily spread south of the Sahara. He also went full out to keep the Americas and Australia in his camp: with an eye to staving off the arrival of Francis' stooges for centuries, he cooked up wild tales of sea monsters and spread baseless fear amongst mariners that those who sailed too far out to sea would disappear right off the edge of the Earth.

Seeing untapped potential in his Asian preserve, Luke hit upon the idea of galloping population growth to increase the use of Chinese logograms. Sadly, illiteracy plagued the rural countryside. He appealed to Gregory the Great for help in the matter, only to discover that the patron saint of teachers was already a firm convert to the ABCs. When Luke showed him how Chinese characters were drawn with brushes and ink, Gregory scoffed. 'Your people need the three R's,' he sermonized, 'not lessons in art!'

Innovations regularly brought new excitement. When Francis de Sales made the acquaintance of a young man named Johannes Gutenberg, it seemed the saint might finally outpace his opponent for good. Moveable type was a stroke of genius. Seemingly overnight, books could be printed at a phenomenal rate. But as Francis soon discovered, the printing press was a two-edged sword: it could reproduce not only text, but images as well. Luke adopted it with glee.

The two saints' rivalry was so captivating that the annual All Saints Day awards ceremony became the most popular event in the celestial realm. No one wanted to miss it. Each year, all of Heaven would wait with bated breath to hear whose name God would call first, Francis' or Luke's. Although strictly forbidden, betting on the outcome became a regular affair, and more than a few archangels were lambasted for using their advance knowledge of the results to amass tidy winnings.

Vying for supremacy, Francis worked tirelessly to develop new needs for the written word. He nurtured newspapers and watched with pride as their word counts soon outstripped those of books. He campaigned energetically in favour of academia, and saw to the adoption of the rule *Publish or Perish*. He cultivated lawyers and trained them in the art of splitting hairs; like virulent pathogens, legalese and legalism spread unchecked, contaminating every facet of civil life. With far-sighted calculation, Francis likewise promoted the use of triplicate forms and fine print, and threw his weight behind an exponential growth in bureaucracy, encouraging technological developments that would lead in time to typewriters and telex machines, mimeographs and photocopiers. He even cooked up alphabet soup.

But Luke was no less industrious. Just when it seemed to many observers that the patron saint of artists was fated to fall by the wayside, he trumped everyone by inventing photography, and cinematography soon after that. The apostle laid claim to both as belonging to the 'visual' arts. In no time, bets were being made that Luke would overtake Francis on the basis of feature films alone, for God accepted that each frame counted as a picture — a whopping 172,800 images for a two-hour flick. Furthermore, every copy was tallied; Luke's numbers went through the roof. It was a minor disaster for Francis, with subtitles and credits offering scant consolation.

Each year, the two saints were neck and neck. No sooner would one contrive a new angle to boost his numbers than the other would concoct a way of leapfrogging higher. When Luke stirred up a rash of new artistic movements and created iconic cults around figures like Picasso and Magritte, Kandinsky and Duchamp, Francis retaliated with a coterie of art historians and critics all hell-bent on writing reams of pedantic commentary. Steamships and aviation and railways gave rise to countless travel books and guides; but globetrotting also spawned maps and postcards and travel posters. Advertising and billboards were a boon for Luke, as were comic strips and coffee-table books. Francis dreamed up writers' workshops and free-verse poetry, and ran ads with AUTHORS WANTED! screamers. With a nod to Saint Matthew, under whose umbrella all use of digits was sheltered, Luke fostered playing cards and philately, and ushered in painting-by-numbers sets. He also took full credit for logos and road signs, and lobbied to replace WALK - DON'T WALK with Ampelmännchen-style symbols for pedestrian-crossing signals. Not to be outdone, Francis hatched Gideon Bibles, classified ads, newsletters and bulk mailings. As for the ubiquitous proliferation of propaganda and pornography, neither platform actually benefited one saint more than the other, although the combined effects of both pushed their scores right into the stratosphere.

The only downside to this unbridled quest for hegemony was a deplorable erosion in standards, since both saints came to privilege quantity over quality. Relegating *Less is more* wisdom to the wayside, Luke and Francis adopted *More is more* as their motto. Worse, shirking the Herculean workload implied by such folly, the two saints threw caution to the wind and instigated a policy of automatically answering all prayers for intercession in the affirmative. The upshot was predictable: authors and artists who had hitherto been rightly and roundly rejected by all and sundry were soon gratified. Cut-rate imprints and vanity presses did a roaring trade; shoestring desktop publishing ventures sprang up in garages and guest-bedrooms; more chapbooks, greeting cards, and picture calendars appeared than anyone knew what to do with. The world found itself awash in images and the written word, and there was no end in sight.

The dawn of the information age, however, convinced the two rivals that a true sea change was imminent. Digital photography had Luke chortling in the corridors. Francis was spellbound by copy and paste. It was no longer a matter of waiting centuries or decades anymore. The time had come:

one or the other was on the verge of being named Saint of the Year. Each believed his ship was about to come in — he would finally eclipse his rival for good and have the last laugh!

❧

Matthew was sitting in the waiting lounge, twiddling his thumbs and eyeing the doughnuts. He looked careworn, poor fellow. He hadn't been sleeping well of late, and he felt distinctly out of kilter. The burden on his shoulders was proving too much. God had asked him to cover all the bases. 'You'll do fine,' He'd insisted. 'You're a whiz with numbers!' Matthew didn't mind so much the lotteries and sweepstakes, the casinos and bingo halls; no matter how many petitions for intercession he received, the Law of Probabilities tied his hands, obliging him to turn a deaf ear. But games of chance were one thing. Binary code was another — nothing but an unbroken stream of zeros and ones from morning till night. Had Matthew known where it was going to lead, he'd have never agreed. Hammering out solutions to computer quandaries these days ate up all his time. Matthew felt trapped. He knew he was neglecting his traditional flock of bankers and bookkeepers, tax collectors and accountants. Scandals had been erupting of late. Books were being cooked, ledgers massaged with legerdemain. His stock-in-trade accountants needed him. He didn't want to be the Binary Saint. He may have risen in the ranks as a result, but quite frankly, he preferred ginger beer to champagne. He longed for simpler times.

46

Yielding to temptation, Matthew reached for a Berliner. As he did so, he caught sight of his sleeve, the one that still bore the traces of Luke's fingermarks. A hundred washings of his ceremonial robes hadn't lightened that shadow. Oh, how he remembered that day! Matthew smiled. As it turned out, that he was sitting here now, waiting to see God, was in no small way thanks to Luke. He patted the sleeve gratefully. It had given him the idea.

The domination looked in.

'The Lord will receive you now,' she said sweetly.

∾

The excitement was palpable in Heaven as the Great Heavenly Hall filled for yet another All Saints Day awards ceremony, the first of the new millennium. Determined to thwart leaks, God had this time put the archangels under lock and key; more, He'd menaced His minions that wagers and bets would earn them nothing but the wages of sin and a one-way ticket to Hell. Security was tight, and the seraphim were making spot checks for 'Go Lucky Luke!' and 'We ♥ Francis!' banners.

The proceedings opened festively with the usual hymn to God's glory. The cherub emcee then warmed up the crowd with humorous anecdotes about the year's bungled intercessions and bassackward benedictions. Finally, God Himself arrived in His chariot, flooding the hall with an impressive effulgence as the thrones wheeled Him to the stage. The time for ranking saints was at hand. All were on the edges of their seats — all with the exception of Luke and Francis, who were preening themselves complacently. Both were sanguine about their prospects for being named Saint of the Year.

Stern and unsmiling, God looked out over the sea of angelic countenances and saintly faces. They were like little children, unable to sit still, waving to each other, whispering to their neighbours. God just glowered, Chin in Hand, waiting for the rustling and stirring of wings and robes to subside. At last, a blessed silence descended on the hall. All was quiet under the celestial dome.

Now He could begin.

'Angels of the Three Choirs, Saints and Apostles — it is My singular pleasure to welcome you to our traditional All Saints Day awards ceremony. This year is no different from any other. For the past year, I have watched with omnipresence and unflagging fascination as you have tended My earthly Garden and nurtured mankind. Every year, thanks to your dedication, thanks to your diligence and your devotion to duty, We manage to keep things on track. Thankfully, you do it for the love of God — for as anyone can gauge from the statistics on votive offerings, intercession these days is a thankless task.'

Smiling to signal that levity was intended, He paused for laughter, but His joke fell resoundingly flat. It suddenly occurred to Him that He'd made precisely the same quip the year before. They hadn't laughed then either. God sighed with consternation and continued.

'Each of you here is charged with responsibility for a certain area of activity. Some of you are content to preside over small but important facets of human life. The humility of Venerius the Hermit, of Saint Lidwina, or of Saint Benedict, should be an example to those of you who keep petitioning Me to add to your list of patronal duties.'

This time, not a few saints and angels let loose with snickers and giggles. But for God it was no laughing matter. He wondered at their obtusity.

'Now, to establish Our annual ranking of saints, the archangels have been working tirelessly, day in and day out, tracking your works, totting up your merits, polling your popularity, recording your intercessions, and — most importantly — measuring the relative weight of your designated sphere of influence. Clearly, some of you will never have an opportunity of figuring among the elite. Know that I love you not less for your lowly stature. You are dear to My Heart, for I cherish good works, no matter how trifling or insignificant.'

An awkward silence met this remark. What He'd said wasn't quite what He meant, but He couldn't take back His Word. Vaguely discomfited, God pressed on.

'Well, I'm sure We're all anxious to learn how everyone's done this year. And what a year it's been! As you're no doubt aware, big changes have been afoot down on Earth. Truly, recent developments have outpaced even Our wildest expectations, and this year, as never before, We have seen the digital era come of age. The impact on your rankings has been considerable. Saints have been rising and falling in unforeseen ways, and We're probably in for a surprise or two. So, let's not hold Ourselves in suspense any longer. Seraphim, bring on the angels!'

Flying off into the wings, the seraphim returned moments later escorting a long chain gang of crestfallen archangels onto the stage. God produced a key. A seraph went to open all the locks, one by one.

'Cheer up, cheer up,' cooed God lovingly. 'Abba hasn't forgotten you. Come, My little ones, come to Abba.'

The archangels stretched their stiff wings and flew to the throne. One drew a sealed envelope from his robes and handed it to God.

'And now, the moment We've all been waiting for,' He announced, slipping His Finger under the flap and tearing it open. He drew out a folded sheet of parchment.

'Angels of the Three Choirs, Saints and Apostles, this year's highest-ranked saint, our newest Saint of the Year, is…'

God unfolded the page. Of course, it was blank. This sort of thing was just done for show. The Most High was All-Knowing and didn't need notes. Feigning disbelief, He whistled.

'Well, well! You'll never guess. Someone We all know and love… someone who is a beacon of assiduousness and tenacity… a saint who has been waiting countless centuries for his chance to step into the holy limelight. Angels and Saints, the winner is —'

The congregation gasped. God looked up.

'I haven't said it yet,' He scolded. 'Why are you all gasping for breath?'

The entire assembly was on tenterhooks, save for two self-assured saints who were puffing out their chests. Both Luke and Francis knew they should appear humble and saintly, but in view of what was coming, neither could refrain from swelling with self-importance.

Once again, God held up the blank page and pretended to read.

'Angels of the Three Choirs, Saints and Apostles! Our Saint of the Year is none other than — *Isidoro de Sevilla!*'

There was a stunned silence.

For a moment, you could have heard a halo drop.

In the stillness, a timorous voice with a Spanish inflection spoke up.

'Who did He say?'

But Francis and Luke were gaping in wide-eyed disbelief.

'*WHO?*' they both blurted in unison.

Like a spark, it blew the powder keg. Out of the blue, pandemonium erupted. Angels and saints of all ranks and levels jumped to their feet, howling in protest. Accusations and recriminations abounded as all bets were called off. It was unprecedented. The seraphim were powerless to restore order. God had never seen such tumult in the heavenly host. A disgraceful scene! But at long last, the furore subsided and most everyone came to his senses. Only Luke and Francis stood their ground. United in rage, they called God to account.

'How can You possibly name *Isidore* Saint of the Year?' Luke fulminated. 'He's been stuck in the bottom tier since the day he was inducted! How could he have possibly earned so much merit?'

'I happen to know for a fact that word use has been skyrocketing,' roared Francis. 'The Internet alone has quintupled in size. Why, I'll bet the archangels can't even keep track of it anymore!'

'And as anyone can see, pictures are pandemic,' bellowed Luke. 'Thanks to clip art and CAD, everyone and their mother is an artist these days. We've got digital cameras on notebooks and phones, and more photo ops scheduled than ever before!'

God marvelled at their brazen effrontery. Oh, how He'd been looking forward to this moment!

'Well, well… to think that I, God Almighty, could be so mistaken. So, your authors and artists have never been more industrious, more productive. Is that it?'

Luke and Francis both nodded vigorously.

'So much so, that words and pictures have beaten out every other activity, bar none?'

The saints were sure of it.

'And that by virtue of this fact, the only two possible candidates for Saint of the Year are Luke the Apostle, patron saint of artists, and Francis de Sales, patron saint of authors?'

The two saints waited expectantly. It was about time God saw the light.

'Well, boys,' said God, 'all that may have been true. Until this year.'

'And why should this year be any different?' Luke wanted to know.

'Because, My dear Luke, nowadays, at bottom, all your pictures — and all your words, Francis — amount to nothing more than a binary stream of zeros and ones, as befits the digital age… *of which Isidorus Hispalensis has been named the patron saint.'*

❧

It was an outcome that astonished everyone, and no one more than Isidore, who was so bowled over that he fell off his chair, then and there. Luke and Francis had to content themselves with being tied for second place, although God was of a mind to disqualify both saints outright for gross misconduct. Their appalling behaviour rankled the Most High. At the end of the ceremony, He made a mental note to review their cases and consider demotion. He was a forgiving god — slow to anger and inclined to overlook things, if only because He missed out on so much of what was going on — but Francis and Luke had gone beyond the pale.

As it turned out, though, Isidore soon discovered for himself why Matthew had begged off binaries. It was mind-numbing, nitty-gritty work. The Doctor of the Church derived no pleasure at all from monitoring endless streams of ones and zeros. As he defiantly remarked to his brother, Saint Leander, 'If I'd wanted drudgery, I'd have signed with the Devil!' Keen to pass the buck, Isidore soon went himself to request an audience with God.

'Isidorus,' cried God with delight as the saint was ushered in. 'How's Our Saint of the Year? What's on your mind, My haloed friend?'

'*¡Caramba, Dios mío!*' moaned the Iberian. He genuflected

hastily and threw himself at God's feet. 'With all due respect, Lord, I have come to beseech You to relieve me of my duties as patron saint of binary code.'

They talked it over. It wasn't his work of interceding on behalf of computer technicians, programmers and end-users that got Isidore down; even if all they ever prayed to him about were computers, he liked patronal duties that involved him with people. And he certainly found his job as patron saint of the Internet to be a worthwhile use of his time; besides, surfing the web in search of broken hyperlinks gave him the chance to mix duty with pleasure. But the business of tracking binary code itself was a bane.

'After an hour or two, Lord, it all becomes a blur. I get so cross-eyed that I end up losing track, and then I have to start all over again. You try keeping them straight! Why, compared to me, Saint Dominic is on easy street,' complained Isidore, in no way exaggerating.

God was sympathetic. Though bound as the Creator to watch over all bytes, great or small, He knew He wouldn't want to have to do the job Himself. Indeed, it was for things like this that He had created the Patron Saints Corps in the first place. But He needed happy campers. Disgruntlement in the ranks served no one's cause.

'Very well, Isidorus. I am willing to release you from the toil of code, so long as We can find someone else to oversee the ones and zeros, if only by proxy. I will give the matter My utmost attention. Will you at least stay on as patron saint for the rest?'

Isidore gratefully consented, and, thus relieved of his burden, took leave of the Holy Presence with an exultant spring in his step.

࿊

God dismissed the chanting seraphim and instructed the domination to hold all calls for divine intervention. He wanted peace and quiet. He needed to think. Mulling the matter at hand, He was annoyed to find that the events of the last few days were still plaguing His Mind. Oh, those two saints! He'd looked into their areas of responsibility. He'd found that, thanks to them, the state of culture on Earth was abysmal. Words had lost their magic, images their awe-inspiring beauty. There was too much of everything now. What the world needed was less, not more. Luke and Francis had let things get completely out of hand; moreover, they were far too full of themselves. A healthy dose of donkeywork was what those two wanted. It might bring them to their senses.

Suddenly, clear as a bell, He knew just what to do. God smiled. It would not only solve His problem with the binary crowd, it would keep His two saints even-steven, and busy to boot.

He called the domination and asked her for parchment and quill. With an almighty flourish, the Lord of Heaven and Earth dashed off a divine decree. He handed it to His winged secretary with a mischievous grin.

'For immediate promulgation,' He instructed. 'I'm naming

55

Francis de Sales the patron saint of ones, and Luke the Apostle patron saint of zeros. See to it that the interested parties are informed, will you? Oh, and please cancel My appointments. I'm taking the rest of the day off.'

And with that settling that, God had the last laugh.

The echo

MANY YEARS AGO, in the town where I am living today, there was a family that lived across the street from the church. The church is one of those medieval edifices such as one commonly finds in our region's quaint, old-world towns. Architectural monument and spiritual counterpoint to life's secular preoccupations, its thick stone walls have been guarding the mysteries of Christendom's faith for centuries, and it has no intention of lowering its guard. Come hell or high water, the church will stand its ground.

The family of which I speak lived in the old half-timbered house that is wedged between the merchant's abode on the right, with its stately façade spanning seven windows, and the doctor's home on the left, distinguished by its fancy brickwork and wrought-iron balustrades. One cannot imagine why such a pitifully small and narrow house should have been built there at all, sharing walls with such grand neighbours, but it was, and it has always been let to people of modest means… much to the irritation of the merchants and doctors who have always lived on either side. One suspects the owner of egalitarian leanings, which is all very fine as a noble point of view, but not something citizens with rank and position care to see acted out next door to where they live.

Like all the other families before and after that have come to live in that house for a spell, the family was poor. That alone was cause for them to be viewed with suspicion by the town's worthy inhabitants. In the morning, the good citizens going about their worldly business would frown when they saw the father arriving in the market square with his bundle to eke out his meagre living selling used books. They would tut-tut with frank disapproval as he spread a threadbare blanket over the cobblestones, on which to arrange his tattered volumes for display, and then settle himself on a wooden crate to wile away the hours reading. No one from the town ever deigned more than a cursory glance at the titles he proposed, but sightseers visiting the region would gladly dawdle and engage him in conversation. Often enough, they would even buy a book or two. Then he would faithfully pay any arrears he might have at the grocer's and go with a glad heart back to his family.

His wife occasionally took in washing, and she was deft with an iron, but most days she devoted herself to baking savoury tarts to sell at midday in the market. Her husband always bought two. She concocted the fillings according to her whims, adding hints of saffron or cilantro, or sometimes ginger and lemongrass, to rouse even the most jaded palate. The tarts were especially tasty, and the townsfolk, though wary at first, grudgingly grew fond of them. It didn't change their attitude toward books, but they were amenable to new flavours.

The parish priest, however, disdained such exotic offerings. He would purse his lips and shake his head, and moralize that earthly pleasures should be simple and plain.

The couple had three children — two girls, aged twelve and nine, and a boy, who was nearly six. The girls had learned wit and intelligence from their father and combined it with a streak of bold autonomy, which they inherited from their mother. It was an admixture that sorely vexed their teachers, for the girls made it a rule to think for themselves and speak their own minds. That gave rise now and then to contentious debate in the classroom. If a teacher dared to present his own view as an incontestable truth, the girls would raise their hands and blithely argue in defence of some other notion — indeed, any notion, even ones that were indefensible, so long as it challenged the teacher's opinion. They seemed to think it an amusing game, and all the more so since they were sure to triumph with their cleverer ways of reasoning; but the teachers complained — it hurt their pride to be bested by girls.

As for the boy, his parents still doted on him, so he didn't go to school. Instead, he stayed at home with his mother in the mornings while she made the savoury tarts. When the baking was done, she would give her son a small box of tarts to carry, and he had to take care not to trip on the cobblestones as the two of them walked through the old narrow streets to the market square. It wasn't far, but the boy was always anxious lest he drop his charge, and always relieved when he reached the square without mishap. Then he would go to see his father.

'Hello, Papa!' he would shout, for all the world to hear.

'Hello to you, Peter,' his father would reply, looking up from a well-thumbed volume of *Das Kapital* or *Don Quixote*. 'Hungry for lunch?'

They would go hand in hand to where his wife was selling her tarts, always pretending that they didn't know her.

'Good morning, Frau Weichwaffel,' her husband might say. 'A fine day for a Blitzruhe, wouldn't you agree?'

'My name isn't Weichwaffel,' she would primly riposte. 'I've never told you my name.'

'Ah,' he would answer, with a wink to his son, 'but that doesn't mean that you won't some day.'

'Don't be fresh,' his wife would retort. 'And I'll thank you to leave the question of Blitzruhe out of our discussions. Booksellers have more sense than you.'

'My deepest apologies, Frau Sowieso, my deepest, heartfelt apologies for being so… so fresh. But if your tarts are as fresh as I am this morning, then I would take two, so long as it pleases you.'

'You mustn't eat them both yourself,' she would scold, slipping them into a paper sack and taking his money. 'You should think of the poor and needy.'

'I wouldn't dare, as you know. Besides, I have my son Peter here to help me.'

'Surely… surely you don't mean… is this your father?' she would exclaim, looking wide-eyed at her son.

And Peter would laugh. He never knew what they were going to invent from one day to the next by way of silly conversation.

Now, one day, walking home together from the market square in the afternoon, Peter and his father had just come to their street when they saw the parish priest emerge from the church's big wooden portal. The priest had no good opinion of his bohemian neighbours, and he gave them a curt nod, glad to have business that meant he must walk the other way. He strode up the street with purpose and turned at the corner without looking back. Peter had never been inside the church. He was curious to know what it contained.

'Papa, what's inside that big house?'

'You mean the church, just there?'

Peter nodded.

His father stopped. He stooped to whisper in his son's ear.

'They say it contains the Word of God. Let's go see if that's true.'

Looking stealthily about the street, as if they should fear lest someone be watching, he led his son up to the big wooden door.

'Now, pay attention,' he explained in a low voice. 'When I open the door, you listen.'

Gingerly taking hold of the iron handle, Peter's father pushed ever so slowly and eased the heavy door open a crack. He looked at his son.

'What do you hear?'

Peter squinted. Beyond the crack, there was only dim silence.

'Nothing.'

Raising his eyebrows, his father stood up straight.

'Nothing? Are you sure? That's odd.'

His father threw the door wide open and strode right in, his son at his heels. Peter was both thrilled and rather frightened as his father pushed the heavy portal shut behind them with a bang. The noise reverberated off the nave's thick stone walls.

Peter reached for his father's hand. His eyes adjusted to the gloom as they made their way down the central aisle. There wasn't a soul in the church. Dozens of votive candles were flickering wanly in a candelabrum that stood before the pietà, set on a dais in a shadowy recess. He looked with grim wonder at the naked man's pallid corpse. Then he saw the crucifix on the wall behind the altar. It looked as though that man were dead too, but Peter wasn't sure. It certainly was a strange house. His father sat down in a pew.

'Perhaps it got out,' he said, making room for his son beside him.

Peter sat down. The hard wooden bench felt cold through the seat of his pants.

'What got out?'

'The Word of God,' whispered his father. 'You see, Peter, every Sunday, the Word of God fills churches everywhere. They get a fresh supply, a whole week's worth. Of course, it's freshest on Sunday, but it keeps pretty well, and it can last an entire week, echoing off these walls. That's why they build churches with an ear for acoustics, so that God's Word can resonate endlessly. It can bounce around inside here for days on end, just as clear as a bell.'

Peter was impressed. But then he frowned.

'But how come we didn't hear it?'

'It must have gotten out. Normally, you slip into church very quietly without attracting any attention to yourself and quickly close the door behind you, so it doesn't get a chance. Then you can sit here and listen to God's Word. It's convenient that way. For example, if you miss coming on Sunday — though you're not supposed to, if you're a Christian — but if you do, you can come here during the week and catch up on what was said. It's echoing all around, every day, unless someone leaves the door open by mistake. Then the Word of God rushes out, and it's gone.'

'Then what happens?'

'Well, then it's windier outside. And they have to wait until the next Sunday to fill the church up again. So they keep the doors closed. Keeps in the draft.'

Peter pictured God's Word rushing out the door, like a dove darting free.

'Why does it rush outside?'

His father smiled.

'Like you, it doesn't like being cooped up,' he said, ruffling his son's hair. 'I mean, look at this place, Peter. Would you want to be trapped in here?'

Peter shook his head.

'There, you see? So the Word of God is always trying to get out. That's why they've got those big heavy doors, to keep a lid on things. If they didn't have those, there'd be a gale outside.'

Peter was looking at the crucifix. The man didn't move. He wondered if they would bury him soon.

'Who's that man?'

'Up there? On the cross?'

Peter nodded.

'Oh, he was a troublemaker. He had a notion that children somehow understood things better than adults. You can imagine where that led. Children started thinking they could have a say. Then their voices were echoing everywhere in here, just like God's. The din was insufferable.'

Peter considered this.

'You mean, if I say something, it'll echo?'

'It will if you say it loudly enough. The rule, though, is that children are to be seen, not heard. That's why we're supposed to whisper, so that things don't get out of hand. But yes, if you shout something, it will echo and echo, just like the Word of God.'

Peter smiled. He liked the idea of his voice ricocheting endlessly off the walls. But then he wondered.

'It that true?'

'I should think so,' replied his father. 'But if you don't believe me, then you'll have to try it someday and find out for yourself.'

'Now?' asked Peter.

'No, not now.'

'When?'

'I don't know. Maybe later.'

'And if you say something, Papa? Would that echo, too?'

'Ah, but I wouldn't do that, you see. I've learned not to say anything.'

His father stood up, and so Peter did too. They walked back

up the aisle to where his father had left his bundle of books beside the holy water fount. Peter looked back one last time, before they went out through the big portal doors and across the street to their home.

Doffing their coats in the narrow entry, they found Peter's sisters sitting at the oval table in the salon, chattering gaily as they did their schoolwork. Their mother was busy in the kitchen.

'Dinner won't be ready for at least another hour,' she announced, stepping into the salon. 'Peter, I want you to go with your sisters and play outside. In fact, I want you to go to the grocer's and fetch me some butter for the potatoes. There now, all of you, out,' she insisted, chasing the girls from the table and shutting their books. Finding her purse, she gave Peter a few coins as her husband slipped his arms round her waist and nuzzled the nape of her neck. 'Off with you now,' she said to the children, 'and don't come back until suppertime.'

So Peter put on his coat again and followed his sisters to the grocer's. For fun, they took a circuitous route and nearly lost their bearings in the town's maze of labyrinthine alleys. It got to be so late that when they finally arrived, the grocer was already carrying his crates of fruits and vegetables in from the sidewalk. Peter gave the coins to his sisters and waited, mulling what his father had said while the grocer made his trips back and forth. The two girls were giggling as they went inside the shop to ask the grocer's son for butter. The poor lad was hopelessly smitten with the older sister. He couldn't help blushing deeply when she looked at him, and he trembled when her fingers brushed across his palm as she gave him the coins. Before she left, he gave her a piece of cheese, so that she would think of him.

But Peter's older sister didn't like cheese, so he got to eat it as they made their way home.

Nightfall had darkened the town, and Peter was trailing behind his sisters when they turned the corner of their street. The two girls ran on ahead, racing each other up to their front door. Peter was too tired to run. He walked instead. As he came level with the church, he saw that the portal was ajar. What's more, he glimpsed the key in the lock. This was a chance not to be missed. He'd be sure of finding out if what his father had said were true. Peter went to the door and peeked inside the gloomy church. Imagining how his voice would feel being trapped inside, he took a sudden deep breath and shouted with all his might.

'Let me out!'

Quick as could be, he pulled the door shut with a bang and turned the iron key in the lock. The mechanism clicked over smoothly. Peter dropped the heavy key into his pocket and hurried home for supper.

෫

The parish priest had just done with locking up the church for the night when he remembered that his housekeeper had asked for his collars. He'd already forgotten them once, the day before, and he knew that if he forgot them again, she'd hound him in the morning when she came to his house. Vociferating a few mighty curses on her behalf, the priest hastily jiggled the sturdy key in the capricious old lock. It was easy to lock shut, but the devil to open — not unlike the Kingdom of Heaven. He set to cursing it too, until it finally yielded. Then he pushed the door open and slipped back inside the church. A lone votive candle was casting an unearthly, valedictory light as he swept past the pietà and made a beeline for the vestiary. There, the priest had just managed to collect his dirty collars when he was surprised by a shout and the sound of a door banging shut.

'What in God's name was that?' he muttered.

Clutching the collars in one hand, he emerged from the vestiary. The candle had given up the ghost, leaving the church dimmer than a tomb. Trying to make his way back through the darkened nave, the priest stretched his arms ahead of himself in a blind search for obstacles, but he still caught a pew in the hip, and he nearly collided with the holy water fount. At last his groping hands found the heavy wooden portal.

'For the love of God,' he swore, discovering it was locked.

The priest throttled the handle for all it was worth and pounded his fists on the door. *'Let me out!'* he shouted, over and over. But his efforts to attract attention were futile. The street was deserted and no one could hear him.

He paced and fumed and shouted some more. By turn piqued and galled, incensed and irate, the priest's formidable reserves of indignation banished sleep. It was the longest vigil he'd ever kept. Dawn found him still marching just as furiously up and down the central aisle, barking his exasperation and clamouring for release.

∾

That night, lying in bed, Peter wondered if his voice would echo on and on, like his father had said. Would he hear it in the morning? The sound filled his thoughts as he drifted off to sleep. Waking once in the middle of the night, he decided he would to go then and there to find out, but he got no further than his room's own door before the night's oppressive cloak of darkness scared him back to bed. So he waited. Only when he saw the day's first light through his window did he dare don his clothes. Creeping downstairs, he got his coat and quietly opened the front door. He stepped outside and looked about. There was neither cat nor mouse to be seen. He felt for the heavy iron key in his pocket. Taking it out, he went across the empty street to the church, where he thought he detected a muffled sound behind the portal even before he slid the key into the lock. But what did he hear when he managed at last to turn the stiff lock and push open the door?

Resounding from deep within the church, resonating off the stone walls and rushing out the door, were his very own words.

'Let me out! Let me out!'

Peter smiled. His father was right.

The tale that had no moral

ONCE UPON A TIME — though I will admit it was a very long time ago — there was a storyteller whose tales always ended with a moral. His stories were instructive and uplifting, and they never failed to teach a lesson a wise man should heed.

The storyteller travelled from town to town, and one day he arrived in a small kingdom's fortified city. Going to the market square, he arranged for the price of a coin to borrow a wooden crate from a vendor. This he plunked down where it suited him best, and he climbed atop to address the crowd.

'Hear, hear!' he called out. 'Let us have a story!'

A few market-goers deigned a cursory glance, wondering what he meant to do.

'Once upon a time,' he began, 'there was a cross-eyed ass named Strabismus, who couldn't see straight…'

The storyteller's voice was rich and melodious, his manner lively and inviting. People paused to listen, and before long they were standing shoulder to shoulder, hanging on his words, eager to hear what would happen next. In search of true love, that silly Strabismus was blithely faltering into one hilarious predicament after another, to the growing delight of the throng. They guffawed at the poor ass's follies, and their hearty laughter caught the ear of the king's son, who was strolling through the market that morning to see what was new and amusing to see. He made his way closer to listen. Risking heartache and headache, the misguided ass was engaged in negotiating a tricky romantic affair with an obdurate fence post, and the listeners were laughing so hard that tears were running down their cheeks. The prince was at first sceptical, but he soon perceived the story's wit. The storyteller went on, weaving the woof and warp of his tale until the hapless ass finally met his God-given match.

'Strabismus had found true love — a creature with long burry ears and an ungainly gait, who did nothing but eat and bray from morning till night. Now, at last, he would know happiness!

'And so you see, dear listeners,' said the storyteller, drawing his tale to a close, 'a cross-eyed ass Strabismus may be, but is he any more so than we? For when it comes to seeking our mate, we are all cross-eyed when blinded by Fate.'

The younger boys and girls laughed merrily and thought it very funny, but the moral brought a rueful grin to the faces of the older men and women. They were the ones who fished a few coins from their pockets and tossed them with a nod of self-recognition into the storyteller's proffered cap — while he, raising his brows in thankful acknowledgement, silently wished them well.

The young prince had enjoyed the story and thought it

would amuse his father to hear the tale.

'Let us invite that fellow to the castle for the evening meal,' he instructed his attendant.

That was how he came to meet the king. Asked to recount the tale of the lovesick ass, the storyteller invented new twists and still more preposterous turns, until the king's face turned beet-red with unbridled mirth. But when he heard the concluding moral, then the king nodded and sheepishly wiped the tears from his eyes.

'Yes, what you say is true,' he commented. 'True indeed.' Shaking off a fleeting shadow of melancholy, the king said, 'Very good, storyteller. Now tell us another.'

And so the storyteller related another tale, but one that was very different — about a kingdom besieged by famine, for all the able men were away doing the king's bidding, and none had been at home to gather in the harvest. Ambitious and greedy, the ruler had mustered his peasants to wage a distant war of conquest; but his plans for quick victory had gone awry: his adversary's forces had succeeded in turning the tables, outmanoeuvring the armed peasants and pinning them down in a cul-de-sac. A drawn-out siege ensued. The trapped men were worn down week by week, until winter came and they had neither will nor strength left to fight. Then did their gaolers strike. Waking from a dream of conquest to a nightmare of defeat, the king watched powerless from a distant ridge as his army was pitilessly massacred before his eyes, his men felled in droves, scythed by swords and pierced by halberds. Horrified, and with the enemy now at his heels, the king fled and in all haste made for the safety of his distant burg; but when he arrived there was no one to greet him. The town was deserted. A vile, sickly stench pervaded the streets, wafting from the open doors of the abandoned houses. Death had been visiting the town in the king's long absence, reaping famished souls for the netherworld. No house had been left unvisited. Rushing to the castle, the king burst into his private chambers and threw back the bed curtains. There he found his queen, her face pallid and gaunt, lying in Death's arms.

'But the grief-stricken king did not have long to mourn his sad loss. His pursuers soon found him, and they made a deadly point of showing him their daggers.

'So it is,' concluded the storyteller, 'that ambitions do trace the course of our lives, and may even serve as guides. But when for counsel greed do we keep, then 'tis own ruin we are sure to reap.'

The king had listened attentively. It was a tale that spoke to a ruler's concerns, and he knew the moral to be sage advice.

The following day, the storyteller was summoned again to the castle. He was taken before the king, who welcomed him with kind words.

'I perceive you to be a man of wit and erudition, though you wear your learning lightly,' he said. 'Your stories have pleased me greatly. They offer wisdom in a guise that even a proud man may hear. If you will agree, it is my wish that you settle here among us, and enter into my service as storyteller to the court.'

'Your Majesty's offer is both generous and enticing,' replied the storyteller with a bow, 'and I am deeply touched. My circumstances have been uncertain for some time now, forcing me to live as a roving wanderer. It is not a life I would care to endure for all my days. I am most grateful for your invitation to live here among your good people, and I should be honoured to serve at your court.'

So it was that the storyteller came to settle in the town, where he soon was esteemed and respected by all for his service to the king. On days when the court was called to session, the storyteller would go the castle's great hall and entertain the assembly with an instructive tale. The stories were often humorous and calculated to put the entire court in a good mood, and the king noted with satisfaction that his councillors would afterwards deal with the realm's affairs with alacrity. But there were also occasions when the court was faced with matters of grave import. Then might the storyteller relate a quite different sort of tale, one with tragic undertones and a cautionary moral, whose wisdom would serve to temper passions and preclude hasty judgement. Thus aided in their deliberations, the king and his court did successfully guide the small kingdom through periods of war and upheaval, peace and prosperity, famine and misfortune, year after year, governing with discernment and astute circumspection.

Indeed, a warm friendship developed between the king and the storyteller, who were close in age. Eschewing his guard, the king would invite his friend to join him for long, informal walks in the woods or nearby fields, or for outings on horseback. In the fall, they would go hunting with the prince, sometimes even leaving for weeks at a stretch. When the time came in the evening to warm themselves round the campfire, the storyteller would regale his royal companions with tales of wolves and bears, of cunning hunters who tracked mythical beasts, of inamoratos who dared risk their lives scaling precipitous crags to steal eaglets for a lady's pleasure. No matter how fanciful or funny the stories were, they always imparted a note of wisdom, and the prince learned many useful lessons.

The years passed in this way, and the young prince grew to be a man; yet still his father, the king, sat on the throne, governing the small kingdom wisely and well. His thick, wavy hair was now streaked with grey and his furrowed face chiselled by time, but the ruler's astute grasp of his realm's myriad threads gave him an unequalled ability to reign. He was at the zenith of his powers.

One day, having dined together at midday, the king and the storyteller went out for an afternoon stroll and soon found themselves walking beside the fields of ripening grain that lay beyond the city's walls. It was a warm, late summer afternoon, but a fresh cool breeze was bantering with the stalks, hinting to those who would hear that autumn was near.

'Did I ever tell you the story of the clockmaker who forgot to set the time?' asked the storyteller suddenly, out of the blue.

'No, you never told me a story about a clockmaker,' answered the king. 'But even if you had, I am sure I would gladly hear it again. Now, pray tell, my good friend — what happened to our happy clockmaker?'

The king was in good spirits, and an entertaining story would surely cap the day.

So the storyteller began. The clockmaker was renowned far and wide for his intricate movements and excellent craftsmanship. His clocks were remarkable for both their accurate timekeeping and longevity, and once set in motion — providing the driving weights were tended to regularly — they would run for ages without incurring the slightest anomaly.

'Now, the clockmaker had a son,' said the storyteller. 'He was a clever lad with a great aptitude for all things mechanical. Yet his father ever regarded him as a boy and only entrusted him with the most trifling tasks in the atelier — polishing pendulums, for example, or fashioning links for the weight chains. Good-natured and modest, the lad never demurred, but in this way, throughout all his formative years, he never learned more than the rudiments of clockmaking.

'The years went by and the boy grew to be a man; yet his father, absorbed in his craft, never noticed. Then, one day, a wealthy patron commissioned the clockmaker to supply the movement for a magnificent clock tower he wished to offer the town. It was to be the largest and most complex movement anyone had ever conceived, with numerous complications — dials to indicate the phases of the moon, the solstices and equinoxes, the dates and months and even the years, for centuries to come.

'The clockmaker set to work on what he knew would be his masterwork, the clock that would stand as an enduring testament to his unequalled expertise. He laboured at the task day and night, filling untold pages with his copious calculations and plans. He was at the height of his powers. He invented ingenious solutions and handcrafted every clock piece himself. All the while, his son worked tirelessly in the background at the few simple tasks his father had taught him — fashioning rods, milling screws, building chains. Several years passed, and the clockmaker, engrossed in his work, hardly noticed. He had never felt happier. Day after day the mechanism grew and took form in his atelier, until one day he set it in motion for the first time. It worked perfectly! Every complication ticked flawlessly along. Now the clock needed only to be carefully disassembled and transferred to the top of the finished tower, which stood overlooking the town's central square. The clockmaker's son offered to help, but the father knew the daunting task had to be perfectly orchestrated; there was too much at stake. Fearing his son might make a mistake, the clockmaker preferred to do the entire job himself. Up and down the tower's twelve flights of stairs he went, day after day, week after week, patiently reassembling the mechanism piece by piece. The complexity was staggering. Only his mastery of the art enabled him to picture how all those pieces fit together in his elaborate plan. But the accumulated years of sustained effort were about to take their toll. On the day the clockmaker ascended the tower to install the final pieces, he felt his heart skip a beat. Sweat beaded his brow as he tightened screws and checked the escarpments one last time. His malaise grew. He felt faint, his legs weakened. He had to grip the handrail as he descended the stairs. When he emerged from the tower he was pale and short of breath. He took a few steps, then abruptly collapsed in the middle of the square. The townsfolk rushed to his aid, his son was hastily sent for. The clockmaker looked up at the magnificent tower. He hadn't yet adjusted the hands of his clock. It was the one thing left to do, before the mechanism could be set in motion. "Take me back up," he rasped. "I must set the time!" But no one dared move him. Then his son arrived and knelt at his side. The clockmaker felt his life ebbing away. There was no time left. "The hands," he choked. The son looked up at the clock and immediately saw what his father meant. "Yes, father, the hands, all the dials," he said. "I see what you mean. Tell me — how do I set them?" He knew that if it were not done correctly, the clock would never work. The clockmaker's eyes widened. Set the hands? For that, one had to know how the clock was made, in all its intricate detail. How could he explain? Just to understand, his son would have to be a fully-fledged clockmaker in his own right, indeed equal to his father. But it would take years to teach him all he would need to know.'

The storyteller paused. They had reached the city gate. The king stood lost in thought for a moment, before turning to his friend.

'And then?' he asked, knitting his brows.

'Sadly, the clockmaker breathed his last and died,' continued the storyteller. 'His son tried for years afterwards to decipher his father's plans, to no avail. He even sought assistance from other clockmakers, yet no one could fathom the mechanism's Gordian workings. The clock was never set in motion. Superstitious people were inclined to see it as a bad omen, and the fortunes of the town soon declined.'

They stood side by side looking out across the golden fields that were rippling and rustling in the gentle breeze. The sun was low in the sky.

'So it is,' said the storyteller — ending with a moral, as was his wont — 'that each generation must learn from the last, lest knowledge withheld is lost to the past. But when fathers to sons do transmit their skill, then from time's certain passing we incur no ill.'

The king was pensive and said nothing. With a discreet bow, the storyteller wordlessly took his leave.

For an entire week afterwards, few saw the king. He withdrew to his apartments and gave instructions that he was not to be disturbed. Once, he summoned his son, who stayed with his father for most of an afternoon; when the prince emerged, the servants saw that he was sombre and thoughtful. Rumours were rife throughout the castle. The king was ill; the king was displeased with his son; the king was planning to wage war; the king had been betrayed by one of his councillors. Nervousness grew, and everyone feared the worst. Finally, word came to convene the court. Summonses were sent to the king's councillors, who made for the castle post-haste. All were anxious. They duly assembled in the great hall, worry etched on their haggard faces as they whispered among themselves. But when the king himself entered wearing his ceremonial crown and mantle, all fell silent, and a deathly hush gripped the chamber. The king, it was noted, seemed to have grown in stature; as he took his place before them, he appeared more determined and more self-assured than ever before. The worthy men were quaking with apprehension as they awaited they knew not what.

'I have called you here today,' announced the king solemnly, 'that you may be witness to the ascension of my son to this throne. From this day forward, my son shall be king of this realm, and I ask you who are gathered here today to pledge him fealty.'

Nothing could have more surprised the guardians of the kingdom. Their eyes widened with both relief and astonishment. The king's son now entered the hall and, bearing himself in a most dignified, kingly manner, went to kneel before his father. The ceremony was brief. The father bequeathed to his son the kingdom and the throne, renouncing henceforth any title to power. Then, lifting the crown from his head, he placed it upon his son's and declared, 'Thus do I crown thee king!' As the son rose, the father and every member of the court kneeled in unison and pledged fealty.

The glad tidings were promptly proclaimed in the city, and word was sent throughout the small kingdom. When the storyteller heard the news, he hastened to the castle and asked to see the king.

'Your Majesty,' said the storyteller, sinking to one knee, 'please accept my wholehearted pledge of loyalty and allegiance.'

'Rise, good master, rise,' answered the newly crowned sovereign with modesty. 'No one knows better than I, that if I am in any way apt to occupy this throne today, it is by virtue of the countless wise lessons you have imparted to me over these many years. I am indeed indebted, and I do humbly thank you.

My father named you storyteller to the court. I should like to appoint you chancellor of the realm, and so make you my closest and most trusted advisor.'

The storyteller was touched by the young king's esteem, but he shook his head. 'Your Majesty, it behoves every man to know the compass of his life. I am by nature a storyteller, and it has been my honour to serve you and your father in this way. Yet a cat is not a lion, and I do not aspire to be other than I am. As you can see, the years have passed for me as they have for your father. Today, I believe I should instead retire from courtly duties in favour of younger, hardier souls, rather than pretend that life is never-ending.'

To this the young sovereign kindly acquiesced, though with genuine regret.

'Then are we to never again hear your stories?' he asked.

The storyteller proposed that he could perhaps return to telling stories in the market square, as he had once done so many years ago, when he first came to the town. This greatly pleased the new king. He ordered that a stonework platform be built there and reserved for the storyteller's use; and he never missed an occasion to join his people in the square, when his attendants brought him word that the storyteller was arriving to tell a tale.

In this way, the former king and the storyteller were able to enjoy their friendship, unfettered by their erstwhile positions. They continued their long walks and outings on horseback, and they went hunting with the king in the fall. Years passed. The father was present to offer gentle words of advice when his son was faced with a dilemma, and sometimes the storyteller would have the young king's ears in mind when he crafted a tale to tell in the market square. The son continued to grow in wisdom and stature, and in time he became the equal of his father. The kingdom's fortunes were assuredly in good hands.

Then, one day, the king's father was taken ill. Age had been gathering the threads of his life, and Death was now preparing to tie the ending knot. The storyteller came each day to sit with his friend. They spoke of memories and times gone by. Both harboured a wistful regret they could not be their youthful selves once again and begin life anew.

One morning, arriving for his visit, the storyteller greeted his friend and asked if he were feeling any better.

The bedridden man chuckled softly.

'You know as well as I there is no cure for life,' he replied. 'These are my last days and hours. But I am exceedingly grateful to spend them in your company.'

The storyteller drew a chair to the bedside and sat down.

'Of what have you been thinking today, Sire?'

'I have been thinking of your stories,' he answered. 'Over the years, you told me so many. I learned so much from your tales. They reminded me of what I had perchance forgotten, and they served to teach me what I did not yet know. They guided my hand in matters both great and small. By the grace of your stories, I became a good king to my people, and a good father to my son.'

With an embarrassed smile, the storyteller demurred.

'Please know, Sire, that if I became a good storyteller, it was by grace of my service to you. You gave me the occasion to rise to the very heights of my craft.'

'Perhaps that is so,' mused the former king, 'unless there is more to it than that. But now, tell me, my friend — I have also been thinking that today I should like it if you would tell me the story of my life.'

It was a request that took the storyteller by surprise. The story of his friend's life?

'Yes, tell me the story of my life,' urged his friend, turning his gaze to the cloudless sky beyond the window. 'I am trying to make sense of it, and I need your help.'

The storyteller felt strangely moved. He hesitated.

'Once, many, yes, many years ago,' he began, haltingly, 'there was a king, and a queen, who reigned over this small kingdom. They were of noble spirit and bearing, and they continued in the steps of their forebears, securing peace and prosperity for their subjects. In time, they were blessed with a son. He was their only child. They loved him dearly, and as the boy grew to be a young man, he knew parental love. He was a serious boy, who loved learning. His father taught him state-craft and diplomacy, as well as how to ride a horse and han-dle a sword; his mother taught him decorum and discretion. He was tutored by men steeped in knowledge, and so learned many arts. The young prince was indeed an exceptional man. But tragedy would force his hand to prove it. A seemingly friendly, neighbouring ruler, basely plotting to seize the small kingdom, invited the king and queen to pay him a visit. They were waylaid and slain as they travelled through the forest. The carefully planned attack was made to look as if it had been perpetrated by roving brigands; but a lone member of the king's retinue, escaping the fray, managed to return and report the truth to the prince. It was in that dire hour that he ascended to the throne. Steeling his courage and resolve, he rallied his subjects to defend their kingdom. But as he led them to meet the duplicitous ruler, the prince concocted a plan to disguise his intent and trick his opponent. He instructed his men to appear festive and gay as they approached the invader's forces, as if they welcomed the news, but to conceal their weapons and wait for his signal. The two parties met on a broad, grassy plain. The prince hailed his adversary as if he were overjoyed to greet him, and his fellows did likewise with the armed serfs, each to a man; and all were taken in by the ruse and soon lowered their guard. Then did the prince with a lightning movement draw his dagger and seize his rival, pressing the tip of the weapon to his throat. His men were just as quick, and not one failed to overpower his chosen target. Raising his voice in an earnest appeal for peace and for justice, the prince detailed the sordid murder of his parents for all to hear and called on the serfs to dethrone their villainous ruler. Whereupon they, truly shocked by what they had learned, united to pledge fealty to the young sovereign. So did the orphaned prince return that day a victorious king.'

The storyteller paused. The dying man closed his eyes and saw with his mind's eye the life he had lived. He glimpsed cherished faces, heard voices from the past. He felt the emotions of grief and triumph that had marked these events, course through his veins once again. It was all as the storyteller told. His eyes still closed, he turned to his friend and waited.

'The king was young, but he had proven his merit,' resumed the storyteller. 'The two kingdoms were merged under his rule, and all prospered in peace and common cause. Among his new subjects, the king found for himself a comely bride, and they were wed. He knew a woman's passion and love. These were days filled with countless small moments of delight, and when a child was announced, his heart leapt with joy. Surely no man was happier than he. But when her time for giving birth came, the labour went dangerously overlong. The young queen bore her husband a son; but she succumbed to her efforts, and paid for her child's life with her own. Then did the king know his darkest hour. His soul fell prey to heartache and woe. In his despair, he yearned to die. But life would not let him go. His newborn son was his heir: the boy would need a father's love and care. Renouncing his sorrow, facing adversity with fortitude and resolution, the king became a man in these times. In his kingdom, too, there were manifold challenges to meet: crop failures, outbreaks of disease, incursions by marauders, influxes of careworn refugees from distant kingdoms that were being ravaged and sacked. The king worked tirelessly to check the tide of misery that had come to bedevil mankind. At last, that dark tide turned. The weary world returned to its senses, a new age of hope dawned. Hardship had matured the king and perfected his wisdom. He now knew that life would ever be so — an endless, varied pattern of fortune and misfortune — and he no longer cared what the morrow might bring. Every day was a gift, and he enjoyed each day fully. His growing son, the apple of his eye, blessed him with filial love. One day, the young prince brought a certain vagabond storyteller to the castle, for the amusement of his father. And he, with greater kindness than any monarch had ever shown to such a doubtful sort, offered that hitherto luckless fellow safety and sustenance. So did the storyteller come to settle here. A warm bond soon developed between the two men, and the king knew friendship. The years continued to pass with an ever-hastening rhythm. When his son became a man in his own right, the king, wiser than most, stepped down from his throne in favour of his son, bequeathing upon him the mantle of power. So did he act in the public weal. Having thus retired from his worldly role, he spent his last years marvelling at the wonder of God's creation and treasuring life's simple pleasures. In time, he discovered he had aged beyond repair. One day, illness took him gently by the hand and led him to bed. And there did he lay — awaiting Death, who comes in the night when no man can see, who comes in the day when no man can know.'

The storyteller had finished his tale. All was silent in the room. His friend opened his eyes. He looked out the window for a long while, contemplating the pale winter sky. Then he turned and sought his friend's face.

'But, what is the moral?' he asked hopefully.

'Alas, Sire,' said the storyteller, a tear rolling down his cheek. 'The tale of a man's life is one that has no moral. The lives of men doth time rescind. Bones and flesh to earth return... and spirit, freed, becomes the wind.'

His friend's eyes filled with sadness.

They waited in silence for a long while. Death paid his visit later that day, as the storyteller was dozing. When he woke, his friend was gone.

The church mouse

THERE ONCE WAS A MOUSE named Timothy, who lived in a church. It was a small church, located at the edge of a small, countryside village, and it was built of grey granite — bone-chillingly cold in winter, yet cool and welcoming on summer days, even days that were hotter than Hades.

It was when he was still just a mouse pup that Timothy had first found sanctuary there, on a morning when he was running to escape the claws and jaws of a determined cat. The village mice sitting atop the low stone wall along the road, opposite the gate, had watched with dread that morning as young Timothy had boldly crossed over and entered the churchyard, intent on having his fill of the rice he'd seen thrown away the previous day. His comrades-in-fur-and-tails had warned him the risk was too great; reminded him that the church grounds were the fief of the village Tom and no place for a mouse who wished for long life; opined that, anyway, the early birds were sure to have gobbled up the last gleanings. But Timothy felt lucky. Youth will do that to you. He went scurrying from one flagstone to the next, sniffing between the cracks. To his great annoyance, he found not a single trace of rice — confounded sparrows! — until, having climbed the steps leading up to the church, he miraculously laid his paws on a solitary grain.

'*Eureka!*' cried Timothy, holding up the proof for all to see.

'*Cat!*' cried the mice, diving for cover.

Sure enough, the dreaded Tom had strolled round the corner of the church. Having looked across the road, he'd seen the mice on top of the wall and followed their gaze to a wee little mouse on the stoop, posing in triumph with his trophy.

'Cat?'

Yes. Cat. More, a cat at that precise instant running full bore towards the steps. But the Tom was old, no longer as fleet as a feline need be to catch a mouse in one bound. Turning tail, Timothy had several split seconds to spare as he scampered to safety through a cranny in the church's heavy wooden door.

Well versed in the tracking of mice, the panting old pussy had settled down for a vigil on the stoop, sure that this foolish young pup would tempt fate sooner or later… but the timely arrival of the parish's stout charwoman — ever swift to harry those known to vent their passions by spraying church walls — had turned the proverbial tables. She shooed the Tom away. Reluctant to abandon easy quarry, he'd tried to slip in behind her through the door; at which point, putting her foot down, the charwoman unceremoniously booted him straight out of the churchyard, so winning for herself then and there an enduring place in Timothy's heart.

Feeling safe in the bosom of the church, Timothy decided to make it his home. The village mice rightly said that poor Timothy was now as poor as a church mouse, for as they all knew, the church had neither pantry nor kitchen, only a tabernacle that was kept under lock and key. Why the tabernacle should have a lock, or why the priest should keep such a tight grip on the key, was hard to understand… after all, Jesus himself had condoned David's eating of the consecrated bread that Ahimelech had given to him. But this was beside the point. Those wafers — so greedily sought after by churchgoers everywhere, so hungrily and thoroughly gobbled up during Mass that no Eucharistical crumb had ever been known to fall by the wayside — were imagined by the mice to be delectable beyond imagining, better than any wafer to be found in any cookie tin. It was to their everlasting chagrin that the matchless prize in the tabernacle trove was sure to remain forever squirreled away.

It is true that the church's sacramental strongbox was as much under lock and key as any other, but what the village mice didn't know was that the charwoman was Timothy's saviour in more ways than one. She came twice weekly, on Fridays and Tuesdays, to sweep and tidy the nave. Is cleanliness next to godliness? If so, there can be no doubt that she was closer to Earth than to Heaven. Indeed, the charwoman's biweekly ministrations were notorious for merely refreshing the scene of the grime — for though her lackadaisical left hand clasped the handle of a broom, her plump right hand was ever clutching a wedge of cake or a cookie. Lumbering between the pews with a rocking gait, she would push her broom ahead and leave a shameless trail of fresh crumbs behind. Truth be told, the only thing about her that worked ceaselessly and with purpose was her mouth. But with Timothy's arrival, the hitherto crumby floor was scrupulously transfigured: following in the charwoman's wake, the hardworking, humble mouse would collect every morsel as if manna were raining down from Heaven in answer to the prayer, *Give us this day our daily bread.* Not only would Timothy enjoy his fill for the day, but there was always a surplus of titbits to tide him over till the woman's next visit. Poor as a church mouse Timothy might be, and those wafers in the tabernacle an unattainable Grail; yet unbeknownst to the village mice, he never went hungry.

The dawn of a miraculously spotless floor, however, had hardly sufficed to placate the church's current priest: his daily prayer was still long on other gripes clamouring for adjudication. Although weak eyesight blinded him to the full extent of her neglect, he nevertheless suspected the woman of near criminal dereliction when it came to cobwebs and dust; and from what he'd heard bandied about in refectories far and wide, his charwoman's delinquency touched on other areas, too. There were rumours that made him cringe. Unwanted imaginings preyed upon his young mind; he lived in squeamish dread of finding himself cornered and compromised in the vestry. Oh, how he wished he could get rid of her! His pleas for intercession, however, were routinely consigned to limbo. The woman had been the present bishop's housekeeper when His Eminence — freshly ordained and straight out of seminary, like all those before and after — had been sent to the parish on his very first assignment. Transferred to the seat of the diocese some years later and earmarked for advancement, he would have gladly taken his buxom broom-handler along, but his superiors wouldn't hear of it: they knew that rising in the ranks required leaving one's beloved housekeeper's behind to push the broom handle for the next appointee. The Church, after all, had its traditions. Nonetheless, the faithful priest, by and by named bishop, never forgot his erstwhile charwoman's rosy cheeks and once shapely rump. Sacerdotal propriety quite understandably precluded him from treating her to the earthly delights of his bishopric, but at least with a sinecure he could pay tribute to his heavenly youth... all those feel-good memories of how, on his behalf and with the innocence of Eve, she had so divinely consummated Jesus' teaching to *Love one another.*

❦

All the same, it was true — the charwoman was careless when it came to cleaning the church. Worse, she utterly ignored the man nailed to the cross hanging on the wall above the altar. Nowhere was her neglect more evident: dark stringy cobwebs adorned his armpits, his arms were covered with a thick tufty layer of dust, and his hair was so ashen-white that younger parishioners swore he was older than Methuselah.

Today was no different. Jesus watched as the heedless, grey-haired hussy trundled off to the vestry to park her broom. Would a sudden hankering for immaculacy stir in her soul? An urge to clean? Would she return, for once, with a stepladder? A sturdy feather duster? A bucket of warm soapy water and a washcloth?

'Of course not,' he sighed, his eyes following her as she returned from the vestry and waddled the length of the nave. He was all too familiar with her ways. Not once in all the years had she ever looked up at him. Not once! Jesus knew it for a fact. It was one of the many drawbacks to his position. He had a bird's-eye view. Saw everything. Heard everything, too… like the fart she let part as she pulled the door open on her way out.

'We'll count that as your genuflection,' he muttered.

The door banged shut, leaving Jesus alone with his thoughts. The road to hell had indeed been paved with good intentions. Why had he bothered to befriend those fishermen in the first place? Hobbled with dogma, hamstrung by precepts, enslaved by a two-faced divinity… it was out of love for his fellows that he'd taken on the mission to ransom their subjugated souls. Why else would he have gone up to Jerusalem, arriving like Isaac on a donkey, to get himself nailed to a cross? A forbidden human sacrifice — signed, sealed, and delivered, right there on Yahweh's front stoop! The silent consent with which their supposedly upright Abba had welcomed the offer was, by Jesus' reckoning, a deal-breaking transgression of the Hebrew Honcho's own Law that could only precipitate one thing: an apocalyptic end — at last! — to the 'everlasting covenant'. *Hallelujah, freedom for all!* But freedom, he discovered, was the last thing his followers wanted. No sooner had his unholy sacrifice paved the way for those knuckleheaded friends of his to throw off the shackles of their old, repressive, soul-numbing religion, than they scrambled to fetter themselves with a new, even more repressive, soul-numbing cult… for which, in a twist that went beyond the pale, they made the instrument of his gruesome death the standard.

The One God had been furious.

'You Nazarethian nincompoop!' He'd roared. 'Look at the mess you've made! Why in My Name did I ever listen to you? *I'll tell them the truth, and the truth will make them free…* Sheer, hare-brained, cockamamie nonsense. I told you, you ninny: they can't hear the truth — their ears are stopped up with stupidity. And now look what we've got on our hands. This is the worst one yet: Christ-inanity. A scourge! I never should have listened to your prayers. Jesus, My boy, let Me tell it to you straight, and from My long experience: you will never free anyone who craves bondage more than love.'

Storming back up to the Seventh Heaven in a fit of righteous fury, the One God went on kvetching to Himself.

'Why am I such a dupe? Every century it's the same… I let Myself get talked into endorsing some well-meaning fool's half-baked scheme to *enlighten* mankind, *free* mankind, *save* mankind… Bah!'

To punish Jesus for having botched so badly, the One God ordained that the Galilean's soul be obliged to invest every single bodily likeness his followers might make of him.

'I'll teach you, you do-gooder, you,' He'd chortled maliciously. 'I won't let you off the cross. By golly, I'll make you rue the day you asked Me for My blessing!'

The wages of sin were death; the wages of being made omnipresent were worse. Crucifixes were hung in every church and on every bedroom wall. Of the two, Jesus couldn't decide which was the more excruciating torture: having to listen to all the pompous preaching that was done in his name and not being able to tell the perpetrator off — *Those Gospels you're using have got it wrong, you dolt! They completely distort what I was trying to do, they misquote me at will… and why do you listen to Paul? He never even met me!* — or having to watch hot and heavy humping going on right under his nose — *O, Lord, how I miss M …and J.* It was Eternal Torment, either way.

'But do You have to throw in the dust and the cobwebs?' moaned Jesus. He threw a glowering glance skyward through the plaits of his crown. His skin was itching terribly. Naileddown hands can't scratch itches.

Jesus wept.

⁂

Timothy peered up from the nave. That poor man on the cross looked miserable.

'I say,' called Timothy solicitously, 'are you all right? Is there anything I can do for you?'

Jesus looked down and spied a wee mouse looking up at him from the central aisle. He had a sudden thought. *Yes! Trade places with me!* But no. That would hardly be charitable. Trade places? Jesus wouldn't want to wish his lot on anyone, man or mouse. If anything, his darn do-gooder conscience would never let him consider it.

'Bless you. It is very kind of you to ask,' said Jesus with heartfelt regret, 'but I don't think there's much you can do for me.'

Then he had an afterthought.

'Unless, perhaps, you could scratch my arms? The dust, the cobwebs… to be honest, the itching is driving me batty.'

Good-hearted and kind, Timothy was more than happy to oblige. Scurrying to the end of the church, he climbed a braided tassel to reach a stonework course and nimbly made his way along the narrow ledge to get closer to the cross. With a deft daring leap and no second thoughts, he jumped the abyss to land on Jesus' toes.

'OW!!!'

The foot flinched violently and began to shudder. Timothy hung on for dear life. *Thank God it's nailed down,* he thought, riding out the spasms. *If it weren't, I'm sure I'd be flung to kingdom come.*

Beads of cold sweat trembled on Jesus' brow. He bit his lip. Being ticklish was his Achilles heel. The nail was driving the point home, making it feel like his foot was being both stabbed and tickled to death. It was several minutes before he managed to calm the storm.

When the tremors subsided at last, Timothy crept warily up Jesus' leg. There was another tricky moment when he reached the abdomen — he could feel the flesh quivering under his claws — but at last he reached Jesus' left shoulder… where he left a track as if he'd wandered off-piste. He was knee-deep in dust.

'Such is the burden I carry,' said Jesus wearily.

Measuring the depths of the situation, Timothy sympathised. It must have taken decades to muster this much downy dirt. Then he thought of his harrowing experience on Jesus' foot.

'You know, you seem to be rather ticklish. Are you sure about this? What if I rub you the wrong way?'

The wrong way? A distant memory caressed his thoughts. Jesus smiled to himself. There was much to be said for doing certain things the "wrong" way.

'What is your name?' he asked.

'Timothy.'

'Yes, my dear Timothy, I am sure. Please, for the love of all that is truly good in this world… scratch!'

The church mouse set to, scuttering along the outstretched arm, scratching and stroking and soothing the itchy skin. The offending dust was swept aside in billowing cascades. Timothy went all the way to the curled fingers and palm, then retraced his steps to continue his ministrations in the other direction. His fears of ticklish tremors were sonorously allayed: Jesus was purring voluptuous moans.

Having swept the arms clean, Timothy now sought to remove the unsightly cobwebs. By clinging to an advantageous crease at each shoulder joint, he was able to lower his tail and flick with expert aim to sever the webs' anchoring strands.

Jesus saw two clumps of spiderweb — first one, then the other — fall with silent gravity into the still swirling dust cloud below. Moments later, he felt a few pinpricks on his skull as Timothy clambered up and over the thorny crown.

'Be careful up there, my friend. Don't impale yourself.'

Timothy's tiny paws tussled with Jesus' thick hair. The indefatigable mouse shook out the dust from the locks and straightened the part, easily sweeping half a century off Jesus' looks. At last, satisfied that he had done all he could, he gave Jesus' ear a friendly tweak and climbed back down.

'I hope you're feeling better.'

Jesus sighed with contentment.

'Ever so much better, Timothy. Thank you. I am grateful. You have brought me relief from my Eternal Torment. You have cared for me like a friend and shown yourself to be truly good, in the same class as saints. Let us not hide your lamp, Timothy. I wish to promote you forthwith to that august rank.'

'Who? Me? A saint?'

'Yes, my good Timothy. You — a saint.'

The mouse was wary.

'Thank you all the same, but I don't see why I should be a saint. Besides, I'm happy as I am. It won't change a thing for me.'

'Oh, but that's where you're wrong, Timothy. Being a saint means you'll have a special power,' enthused Jesus, 'one that only you will have. Just think of the votaries who'll look up to you. You'll be able to answer their prayers by the power of your gift.'

'A special power?' queried Timothy. 'What sort of special power?'

Having seen in his time quite a few mice trying to pull off a Host heist in vain, Jesus had an inkling of what sort of power a mouse might put to good use.

'Timothy, I propose that you have the power to open the door of the tabernacle whenever you want, without a key. All you will have to do is imagine a key, and the door will open, as if by magic.'

Timothy's eyes widened.

'Yes,' said Jesus, 'as if by magic. And you know what's inside the tabernacle, don't you, Timothy?'

The mouse could hardly contain himself.

'—*the Cookies!*'

Jesus smiled. Timothy was jumping up and down on his shoulder like an excited child.

'Yes, Timothy, the *consecrated* Cookies. And you'll be able to eat them all, as many as you like.'

Jesus instructed Timothy to climb down and make his way to the altar. It wasn't every day that he got to make someone a saint, and he liked to mark the occasion. It was something the One God hated, of course, but He had overlooked proscribing the prerogative when He had dished out Jesus' just deserts.

Gingerly tiptoeing to the centre of the altar, Timothy stole a glance at the tabernacle, which stood on a small table alongside the wall. He could hardly wait. With becoming solemnity, Jesus looked down and spoke true.

'Mouse of uncommon humility and generous spirit… I hereby name you *Timothy, Patron Saint of Poor Church Mice*. Upon you I do bestow *The Blessed Power To Open Tabernacles At Will*.'

♋

Timothy woke early the next morning. He was quite conscious that his whole life had changed overnight. He, a saint! With a special power!

Emerging from his burrow behind the wainscot in the vestry, Timothy entered the nave with both excitement and trepidation. He looked up at the crucifix. Jesus seemed at peace. And fast asleep, too. *Thank goodness for that*, thought Timothy, ruefully stroking his tail. The night before, by the ruddy glow of the sanctuary lamp, Jesus had waxed lyrical about his days as a miscreant messiah and reminisced at length about his Galilean followers' many foibles. For a mouse, such talk was only vaguely interesting; after sitting on his haunches through more than half a dozen tales concerning the disciples, Timothy had frankly had enough — his tail was getting sore. But Jesus was in a gay mood and wanted to burn the midnight oil. His itching had been relieved; now he was itching to talk. Wary lest his benefactor renege on the Cookies, the poor mouse had had to reconcile himself to a sleepless night. He'd grinned and borne it stoically… like a saint.

Timothy went to the small table and shimmied up a leg. Reaching the top, he peeked over the edge. Standing along the wall like a miniature mausoleum was the tabernacle. It was of simple design, fashioned of wood, its bronze door decorated with bas-relief sheaves of wheat. The door was locked, of course; but even if it hadn't been, without a key it couldn't be opened: there was no handle to pull, and the thinness of the gap round the door would have stymied even a mouse's fine claw-tips from gaining purchase. These inviolable repositories had thwarted mice for millennia.

Timothy climbed on to the tabletop and approached the tabernacle with chary awe. On the one paw, he was half filled with doubt — it looked impregnable. On the other paw, he half believed what Jesus had told him would happen. All he had to do was imagine a key to fit the lock? Very well. Trembling with anticipation, the mouse set his mind to conjuring a bow and shank. Nothing happened. Not enough? In his mind's eye, he pictured a bit with its wards and joined it to the shank, forming thus an entire key… and instantly a click was heard. Right on cue, the tumbler turned a full quarter clockwise in its cylinder, and with soundless solemnity the door swung open just as Jesus had said it would. As if by magic.

Timothy saw a small ciborium inside, covered with a white linen handkerchief. First, he threw a cautious glance round the empty church. Then, creeping forward, he reached for the veil and pulled it aside. Before him, lying in the bowl, was the Body of Christ — a tidy pile of white, tiddlywink-like wafers.

Timothy lifted the topmost wafer from the stack, opened his mouth, and bit the Host. His eyes widened and he gagged.

'*Yecch!*' he spluttered. He spit out a mouthful of dry, flavourless crumbs.

Timothy looked with horror at the wafer. *This* was the Consecrated Cookie? The Holy Grail of hungry mice everywhere? No butter, no fat, no sugar, no egg, no salt, no seeds… if only they knew! No wonder it was so pale. It was Tasteless. Anaemic. An Unpalatable Joke.

'Criminy! Who in God's name would ever want to eat this

pap? Banish the thought!'

Throwing the tabernacle door shut, Timothy turned tail. He wouldn't be needing that imaginary key. Nor would he bother himself again with that man on the cross.

'Let him talk the tail off some other mouse,' he grumbled, climbing down from the table.

Duly chagrined, Timothy returned to his burrow… empty-pawed, but a much wiser mouse.

❧

Two days later, the charwoman returned to sweep the church. Timothy had been awaiting her arrival with as much longing and anticipation as if he'd been on the lookout for the messiah. Following her out of the vestry when she came to fetch her broom, he was delighted to see that her other hand was clutching a deliciously crumbly scone, filled with currants.

The poor church mouse gave thanks to the One God above. Between the Blessed Sacrament and a Buttered Scone, there could be no doubt as to which came from Heaven.

Death's watch

'We'll be going this way, if you please… Come along … Thank you… That's right, like a good fellow… I'm here… Yes… I'm happy to guide you…'

The old curmudgeon stopped in his tracks.

'Bollocks. You didn't answer my question. Where are you taking me?'

Every now and then, an errand put Death's patience to the test. This one had been digging in his heels since they'd left the house.

'I told you, to a wonderful place.'

'I heard that. But you didn't answer my question: where *is* your wonderful place?'

Death traded in euphemisms. All were trite from overuse. New ones were hard to come by.

'Just round the next bend. Just over the hill. Just past the corner.'

'I'll bend your corner, you hill of beans. You're a hoodlum. I don't like you.'

Oh, these long, drawn-out departures. What did they think to gain by it? Eternity? He liked it best when they were chipper and curious, game for a lark. Children were like that. They could be so inquisitive. It was fun to talk with them. Death savoured their spirit. He always found their passing poignant. But the older errands were a mixed bag. Some were complainers — they'd talk your ear right off with hard luck stories and endless self-pity. With them, the silence afterwards came as a welcome relief. Others were happy enough to forget their tribulations, glad to be rid of past burdens. Chortling *Thank God that's over,* in a trice they'd be reliving the high points of their life, rattling on and on as they snickered gaily about good times gone by. Death and his errand would stroll side by side like a pair of old chums, wending their way round the next bend, over the hill, past the corner. There was never any hurry… but still, when the moment felt right, Death would slow his pace, then turn and wait. The soul he'd come for would stop as well. They were so beautiful then, relieved of the cares and worries that had plagued them in life. Their face would shine. They'd become once again the happy-go-lucky soul they were at heart, the person they'd always been deep down, underneath the façades they'd clung to all their lives for appearances' sake, behind all the barriers they'd erected to protect themselves from hurt. Death would regard them with a beatific smile. His errands then were more loveable than ever. Reaching out like a lifelong friend, he would encircle them with his arms and draw them close for a heartfelt hug, wrapping them snugly in the embrace of his heavy black cloak. It was a fine way to go.

A cavilling croak overtook Death's reverie.

'…and if you want my opinion, I think you've no right to drag me out of bed like this in the middle of the night. I'm a sick man. It's chilly out here. I should be in bed, you know — under the covers!'

Death fixed his charge with a gaze of wry deference.

'Are you cold?'

The old man started. He hedged.

'I want my scarf. At least my scarf, if you're going to keep me out like this.'

'I asked if you were cold. Are you cold?'

They were never cold. Never hot. Never in pain. Never hungry or thirsty. They were free of all that. Free of all earthly cares and bodily woes. For the first time in years, in perhaps all his life, the curmudgeon — bane of his family, vociferous scourge, loather of mankind — found himself dumbstruck. He was afraid.

Death couldn't resist.

'Cat got your tongue?'

His errand licked his lips.

'Don't like cats,' he said, glancing around uneasily. It was as if he were looking at the world for the first time. 'It's… it's actually not that chilly.'

Beyond the trees, the stars twinkled. The old man squinted at the sky.

'Say, there's a moon up there. Looks lovely.'

It sometimes happened like that. A person who had been asleep his whole life would finally wake up. Long overdue, but still… the moon was indeed lovely, and the old man saw it. His weatherworn lips flickered with a fleeting smile.

'Lovely indeed,' concurred Death. But it was getting late.

'That watch of yours,' said the old man suddenly, as though reading Death's mind. 'What time does it say now?'

'Ah yes, my watch…'

Death fished for the timepiece in the folds of his cloak. The hands would be aimlessly spinning in circles, he knew, but he gave it a glance for show.

'Oh, it's quite past midnight,' he replied.

'Let me see that thing,' said the old man testily, himself once again. 'I don't trust you. It was only just midnight when you dragged me out of bed.'

Death passed him the watch. It was time.

'What? This thing's all wonky. There's a screw loose here… Hey!'

Death had stepped forward and was extending his arms to engulf the old man with his cloak.

'Back off, you!'

The black cloak closed round.

'Help!'

A surprisingly fierce struggle ensued. Those who had spent their earthly years cursing and hating life were often the most tenaciously opposed when it came to letting it go. The old man's will to live was no easy thing to smother. Death tried to get his cloak in place. He had to utterly block out the world, shutter every last chink, cork every last peephole. Subduing the old man was good sport, though; Death didn't mind. The outcome of the contest was never in doubt. Death always won. No soul could fend him off forever.

'*No! No!*'

Inside the cloak, gripped with panic, the old man was thrashing and kicking like a bronco. The overpowering darkness was nearly complete and he was wild with terror. Then a gap in the folds suddenly appeared, close to the ground. Desperate, he made an all-out lunge for it. As his face hit the earth he lost hold of the watch. Was he free? He thought so… for an instant, at least. Looking sideways through the grass and the scattered autumn leaves, he spied the watch lying on the ground a little ways beyond the utter darkness that came softly down like an opaque curtain, obliterating his spirit.

ℰↃ

The boy cradled the watch in his palm. There was an engraved inscription on the back that appeared handwritten.

If it weren't for you, My friend, where would I be?

He opened the case once again. The face was quite odd — bony white, and the hours were marked not with numerals, but with miniature granite-grey stelae. The hour and minute hands showed a little past two. That was wrong, of course; he'd only just had breakfast. Seeing as how the slender red second hand didn't move, though, it was easy to deduce that the watch needed winding. His father had a pocket watch like this and had let his son wind the spring many times, so the boy knew all about watches; it was probably why he'd always wanted one of his own.

Finders keepers, losers weepers? Feeling grand about his good fortune, he turned the crown a few times and pocketed the treasure, humming a tune as he went on his merry way to school.

During the morning recess, the boy went off by himself to a corner of the schoolyard and took the watch out of his pocket. The second hand had advanced a little ways, but it still wasn't ticking freely. A bit more winding would remedy that, he thought; he felt the crown engage with the mainspring and gave it half a dozen good turns while surveying his classmates at play. When he looked again, he was disappointed to see that the red needle was just as stationary as before. Thinking that the mechanism might free up if he advanced the hands, he pulled out the crown and began twirling it clockwise. Out of nowhere, Sally suddenly ran up and gave him a furtive kiss on the cheek. The boy was taken aback. What had gotten into her? So far as he knew, she was in love with that horrid Thomas. At least, she'd been so since the end of September. They were always holding hands.

The surprise of Sally's kiss caused him to let go of the crown. He just happened to look down and caught sight of the minute and hour hands whirling backwards. They came to a stop at a little past two. That was odd. Then, looking up again, he saw Thomas and Sally over beyond the swings, kissing. That too was odd, given that she had just raced over and given him a kiss on the cheek. He was as confused as to why Thomas hadn't noticed what she'd done as to why she should do it in the first place.

When he got home that afternoon, the boy went upstairs to his room and took a good long look at the timepiece. Nothing had changed, except that the second hand had advanced and was now pointing to the nine o'clock stela.

Fiddling with the crown, the boy tried advancing the hands again. The minute hand spun round and round — and suddenly, he was flushed with a delicious recollection: kissing Sally! They'd kissed that very afternoon, not long after school, for the first time. But… that couldn't possibly be. Yet he was sure of it, just as sure as he was sitting on his bed. Clicking the crown into place, he let his eyes wander and was startled to see fresh green buds on the branches outside his window. Getting up to look, he discovered that the autumn leaves he'd shuffled his feet through that morning on his way to school were nowhere to be seen. Still more inexplicably, there were daffodils blooming in his mother's flower bed. It was then that it hit him: the watch had advanced the time.

'Wait a minute!'

He didn't want to miss that kiss. Pulling out the crown, he ever so carefully turned it counterclockwise, just a tad.

'Hurry up, up there,' called his father. *'You're late for school.'*

The boy looked outside. Sure enough, the sun was rising in the east. Leaving the watch on his desk, he grabbed his book bag and ran downstairs.

He walked to school that morning with a keen desire to savour the day. The furtive kiss that Sally had given him in the schoolyard had occurred a week beforehand. He recalled that he'd dared to invite her out after school on Friday, and that they'd walked together to the ice cream shop. He remembered that while she was having a hard time deciding what flavour she wanted, he'd gone ahead and ordered his cone; then, saying that for her the weather was still too cold for ice cream, she'd ordered hot chocolate instead, with marshmallows. He'd felt like a fool. He envied her for choosing hot chocolate. He'd never even noticed it on the menu. They talked of school and gossiped about their physics teacher, but what he really wanted was to ask her why she'd run up and kissed him earlier in the week; yet he didn't have the nerve, and she didn't mention it. He fantasized that he might get a chance to hold her hand when they walked home together afterwards, but that didn't happen, either: as soon as they'd come out of the shop and felt the cold wind, she'd put her hands in her pockets.

But today, he noticed that Sally was making eyes at him when they passed each other in the hall, and during recess she came up and asked him to meet her after school, behind the gym. It was then that he noticed Thomas keeping to himself; when Sally crossed the schoolyard on her way back to class, Thomas looked away; then, once she'd passed, he looked back and stared after her. He seemed forlorn. The boy couldn't help but feel a wee bit self-satisfied, and cautiously cocky. The end-of-school bell rang at last. The boy decided he should take his time getting to his tryst with Sally. He didn't want to seem over-eager by arriving before she did. Unfortunately, his history teacher waylaid him in the hall and asked for his help, and by the time he could finally get free, he was more than overdue getting to the gym. Sally was nowhere to be seen. Cursing his history teacher, incredulous that he'd missed his rendezvous, the boy headed home, dejected and thoroughly confused. He was looking mostly at the ground as he walked on the path that led through the small wooded area behind his neighbourhood, so he didn't see Sally approaching him until the last moment. Without saying a word, she reached out and took his head between her hands as she kissed him full on the mouth, slipping her tongue between his lips. The boy was overwhelmed. His tongue touched hers, his hands sought her waist, he drew her close. It lasted only long enough to whet his desire, before she pulled herself free and smiled at him.

'You're cute,' she whispered. Then she ran off.

That was the kiss.

His first kiss.

❧

The boy relived that day eight times. One after the other, eight days in a row. Returning home afterwards, he'd find the watch on his desk exactly where he'd left it and he'd remember everything about having set the time back. But though he deliberately reversed the hands knowing he would get to re-live Sally's kiss, once he was back in the earlier time he would completely forgot what was coming. The only difference was that in the course of the day, he would be struck now and then by an acute sense of déjà vu. He was still unavoidably waylaid by the history teacher, and he always cursed when he arrived late at the gym, yet he met these frustrations with ever-greater detachment. The contretemps were taken in stride, their sting dulled by a vague familiarity; but he discovered by the same token that his pleasure in Sally's kiss was rendered less keen as well. When for the eighth time running she kissed him full on the lips, his attention lazily focused on the muscular thrust of her probing tongue. What had at first seemed limitlessly wonderful was not borne out by endless repetition.

The next day, for the first time in over a week, the boy did not reset the time. Instead, he secreted the watch in a good hiding place and went to school. When recess came, he looked for Sally and saw her by the swings, laughing and talking with her friends; he felt shy about joining the group, but she waved and called his name; and when the bell rang, she took his hand in hers as they all walked back to the buildings, and everyone in the schoolyard saw it, even Thomas.

Things went on this way for more than a month. Sally was unabashedly affectionate in public. The boy was thrilled. Now and then, he'd use the watch to backtrack a day or two, to relive an especially nice moment with her. On a few occasions, he even skipped ahead, eager to peek round the corner into the next week; but each time he did so, he'd realise he had missed something fun that had happened in the interim. Since each passing day seemed to bring a delightful new development, he soon was just content to let nature run its course as time intended, day by day.

Their courtship reached a climax with an afternoon spent

together on the eve of their end-of-term finals. It was Sunday, and her parents had left for the day on an outing with her younger brother. Sally had begged off, saying she needed to study; as soon as they'd gone, she'd called and told him to hurry over.

Arriving as quickly as he could, he found her waiting for him on the path she knew he'd take through the woods. She gave him a kiss.

'Follow me.'

Sally led the way, trailblazing a shortcut to her parents' backyard. At the edge of the garden, she stopped short to check if the coast were clear. Then she took the boy's hand and made him run with her across the yard, straight into the sunroom at the back of the house.

Since the exams were looming and couldn't be put off, the boy had thought they were at least going to do some studying together; he'd brought his class notes to compare with hers. But Sally had no intention of wasting time with trigonometry or the Russian revolution. Drawing him to lie down with her on the spacious rattan sofa warmed by the sun, she snuggled herself in his arms. As they cuddled and spoke of silly things, he began to timidly explore her beautiful face, running his fingers along the line of her chin, the swirl of her ear, the contour of her lips. She took his hand in hers and pressed his palm to her chest. He could feel the rise and fall of her breath, the faint pounding beat of her heart. She waited. He didn't know what to do. She pulled his shirt free from the waist of his pants and ran her hand up underneath, caressing his chest. It was then that the boy awkwardly dared to see if she'd let him unbutton her shirt; it was something he had dreamed of doing, but he hadn't imagined it might happen this soon. She was wearing an old button-down shirt of her father's. His fingers closed round the first button. He noted that Sally made no move to stop him. Instead, looking down, both she and he watched as his hand clumsily undid each button, one by one. The body of the shirt parted ever so slightly, revealing her belly and the cups of her bra; and as she buried her face in his neck, he watched his hand slide up and under the edge of her shirt, his fingers extended in search of her breast. His palm cupped the padded mound and squeezed it softly; her lips sought his; they were kissing on the rattan sofa; her arm held him firmly round his waist, under his shirt. The afternoon sun pursued its course and they pursued theirs. When she tired of kissing him, she reached to unclasp her bra and boldly pushed his face to each of her nipples. Her hands were grasping and pulling his hair as he nuzzled her breasts and suckled their points. Then, resting his cheek on the soft flesh of her tummy and eyeing her waist, he paused to wonder if she'd let him go further. He was just about to test the top button of her pants when the muffled sound of the front door opening and Sally's parents calling her name suddenly sent the boy dashing headlong out of the sunroom on a panicked flight across the backyard and into the woods.

When he got home, still giddy from his narrow escape and tingling with unquenched desire, it hit him that he'd left his notes behind. The exams! The boy groaned. It was the last thing he wanted to think about. They were scheduled to last the whole week. He'd hardly get a chance to see Sally, what with all the last minute studying. And the following weekend, his oldest cousin was getting married; his parents were adamant about attending the wedding; they'd be leaving directly after school on Friday and wouldn't be back until late Sunday. Boredom guaranteed! It was too much. And too long to wait.

The boy went upstairs to his room and gratefully retrieved the watch from its hiding place. Thank God for this magical treasure — it was going to spare him an entire week of mental exertion and pleasure postponed. Pulling out the crown, he gingerly advanced the movement until the memory of his cousin's wedding arose fresh and vivid in his memory. They'd just gotten home. The exams were over; thinking back, he recalled that Sally had given him his notes when she'd seen him the next day; he also recalled that she'd acted strangely distant. He'd chalked it up to her being nervous about the finals. Later that morning, when they had their history exam, he'd waved to her as she came into the auditorium to show that he'd saved a desk for her next to his; but she'd shaken her head and gone to sit instead near the opposite wall. This time, he'd chalked it up to her not wanting to be distracted. But the whole week had gone like that. He'd only managed to talk with her once, just before their English exam, when they were waiting in the hallway; and she'd been unaccountably vague, as though she were somewhere else. He had no idea why. She turned in her exam paper early and was the first to leave the auditorium, and he didn't see her again after that. Altogether, the boy now remembered that he'd lived through a terrible week.

The next morning, setting off through the woods, he decided that Sally must have been especially preoccupied with passing her finals. They sure hadn't studied much that afternoon. She'd probably been trying to make up for it by redoubling her concentration. Coming to a fork in the path, it crossed his mind that he might be able to intercept her on her way to school. With luck, they could kiss and fondle a bit; if not, it would just mean he'd walk a bit further than usual. He followed the path a short distance through the woods. As he neared the next junction, he saw two people up ahead locked in a passionate embrace. He smiled to himself: that was exactly the sort of kissing he'd soon be enjoying with Sally. Blithely unaware, engrossed in each other's lips, the two lovers were clinging to each other in such a way that as the boy approached, he had the vicarious pleasure of watching the fellow knead the girl's rump.

Then a twig snapped under the boy's shoe, and the girl turned round with a start.

☙

It was an unspoken rule: they should never discuss whose power was the greater. For the sake of their friendship, and to ensure their get-togethers would always be cordial and relaxed, both God and Death studiously avoided broaching the subject. They could talk about anything else, but never that.

For his part, Death took simple enjoyment in God's company, but God was filled with the profoundest respect for Death. He knew He owed His friend an untold debt of gratitude… for without him, there could be no Life. Creation alone was not enough. The universe? A cranked up chemistry experiment — fascinating, to be sure, and boundlessly immense… yet fatuously inanimate. Unceasing expansion into an unknowable void reflected its Maker's immeasurability, but so what? Compared to *Life*, mere infinity was nothing. No, it was his friend Death who made Life possible — though God, prideful as He was, had no intention of acknowledging the fact by admitting it openly.

On Earth, of course, He was given full credit for Creation; that was unquestionably His due, hands down. Could He help it if humans mistook their big Abba in the sky for the source of life as well? They were so simple-minded. They amalgamated everything. Not that He saw any reason to correct them. They'd eventually wise up. It was His policy to intervene as little as possible. With a wry grin, Death would sometimes raise his eyebrows at this, but he never complained about being passed over. Quite unlike God, Death was unassuming. True, he cultivated ingenuousness, but his self-assurance was rooted in the very core of his being. He was utterly free of doubt. Again, unlike God.

Free of doubt, yes, but conscious that he didn't know everything. Death's domain was the essence of life; the Petri dish in which to spawn it, though, belonged to God; Death would instil the innate life force at the very start, whereas God ran the rest of the show from that point on, the material trappings that gave an individual life structure and form, trajectory and spatial coordinate. In this lay His omniscience. Although lazy most days, if He put his mind to it, God could keep track of everything. His motto was *If it's made of matter, it's Mine* — and that amounted to every *thing*, and thus, seemingly, everything. Everything, that is, save the immaterial soul.

Death didn't mind, only it sometimes put him at a disadvantage. Like today. He and God had met to compare notes, as they often did; and while nothing had been said outright, their conversation still left him with the conviction that God knew about the watch. Indeed, had probably always known… even from the start, so many years ago.

Insofar as that went, Death had realised it for himself a short while after. He'd gone to fetch a young girl whose time had come, and since he knew that children loved playing with the watch, he'd wanted to brighten her last moments. Yet the watch was nowhere to be found. Happily, the girl had laughed merrily at seeing this funnily attired character turn round and round like a whirling dervish, patting himself in every which way, searching for a nonexistent something in the folds of his cloak. She'd found his antics hilarious. Death was glad for that; it gave his discomfiture a silver lining; more, the girl had left the world with a smile on her face.

Returning afterwards to the woods where he'd tussled with the old man the night before, Death had turned over every autumn leaf in his search for the watch. To no avail. Someone must have found it, filched it. God only knew where it was. And that irked Death. God was proud, but Death was lofty, and disliked being shown up.

So he never mentioned it. God too said nothing about it.

Death wondered: was his friend genuinely in the dark, or just feigning ignorance? With God, you could never be sure.

Over the years, they'd returned many times to the tale of the curmudgeonly old fart. When things were slow, it was good for a laugh. Yet on this particular occasion — what with wars being waged in several hot spots, rampant diseases scything down broad swaths of humanity, famines afoot on two continents, firearms circulating unchecked, and fresh corps of kamikazes running amok — there already was much to discuss. Death hadn't anticipated bringing Time to a standstill for any longer than was necessary before hurrying back to Earth to reap the next harvest.

Nothing doing: waving mayhem aside, God had pressed His friend to tell the story yet again. Death obliged, grudgingly, knowing that in any case, he wouldn't be able to leave until he'd fulfilled his friend's wish; a dogged bent for getting what He wanted was a hallmark of God's nature.

No sooner had Death begun mimicking the testy old man's *I'll bend your corner, you hill of beans*, than thunderous peals of laughter were heard reverberating off the dome of Heaven. Tears streamed down God's bearded Face. Guffawing and slapping His Knee, the old divinity's mirth was so great that He probably would have wet Himself had the angels not brought in a chamber fount. God howled as Death related his errand's objection that *This thing's all wonky. There's a screw loose here!* — and when the old man's face hit the ground, God stomped His Feet with glee. He nearly split His Sides, He was laughing so hard.

'Oh! Oh! Stop! No more. I tell you, it's too much…'

The angels flew away with the pot, taking care to keep it level, and went to sprinkle the holy waters on an unsuspecting patch of desert somewhere.

God wiped His Brow and sent a seraph out to rustle up some refreshments.

'Ambrosia, My good fellow, ambrosia! And don't forget the libations. Oh, that watch. It'll be the death of Me. *There's a screw loose here… Ha!*'

Death smiled, but eyed his friend. Why so much laughter? He'd heard the story before. It wasn't new.

'I'm *so* glad I thought to give you that watch.'

That settled it. Now he was sure. God was playing him for a fool. *He* knew. More, He knew Death *didn't* know. That watch was somewhere. In whose hands? Into what kind of mischief had it gotten the hellion? It was a potent timepiece, not to be trifled with. God had given Death the watch to ease his troubles with recalcitrant errands who refused to believe their time was up, who wouldn't put to rest their dogged will to live. In the past, Death had had to gently pry their fingers from the sheets, cooing wishy-washy things like, *'You're not getting any younger. Believe me, you've had a good spell of fun. When you've been around a few times, it's not the same anymore.'* And still, they'd hang on for dear life. He'd seen more good sheets ruined that way than a ragpicker could salvage. Yet dash it all, they had to let go if they were going to leave. Death had grown tired of having to coax them along. So God had hit upon the idea of the watch and given it to Death as a present. It did make his job easier. When his errands looked at the time, the hands would spin steadily round the dial, only slowing to a feeble crawl as they neared midnight. 'You see,' Death would gently enjoin, 'the hour is nigh.' Resignation would creep in, unbidden but ineluctable. They would hand Death the watch, take one last look round, and bid life farewell.

'Yes, I have always been grateful for Your gift. I won't say it succeeded in convincing our old sourpuss it was time to move on, but then, he had a screw or two loose.'

'Well, We can at least be glad he didn't drop it while the two of you were scuffling,' said God disingenuously as the seraph returned with a tray. ''Twould be a crying shame if that watch were ever broken.'

A freshly concocted batch of golden ambrosia was heaped on a platter.

'Oh, you sweetheart, you! Look what you've brought us… and nectar, too!'

Death reached for a goblet.

'Don't mind if I do.'

'Here's to you, My friend,' said God, raising His own in a toast. 'Hallelujah!'

With a meaningful wink, He added, 'After all… if it weren't for you, where would I be?'

⁂

Returning to Earth, Death furrowed his brows. He was no fool; he could read the dregs in a chalice, the crumbs on a platter. He had every reason to surmise he would soon find his watch. Still, it annoyed him when God toyed with him. That they were like Siamese twins was a given; no less than yin and yang, darkness and light, good and evil, they were bound to each other. You couldn't have one without the other. They were equals in every way. Yet there He was, God in Heaven, sitting on His laurels, slurping nectar and munching ambrosia and keeping Death in the dark, playing games and laughing up His sleeve. It was irksome.

✑

The years had passed. All of the years. He'd relished good fortune. He'd bypassed the bad.

The watch had been a lifelong habit. When he'd liked his life, he'd lived it day by day. When he hadn't, he'd skipped ahead. He'd accustomed himself to good times. Not for him, rough seas, muddy waters, marital discord, daily grind, dead-end boredom — when those had come along, he'd gotten out the watch and given the crown a few turns till he hit on something better. Now and then, life had surprised him with a stellar moment. That was something he'd relive to the hilt, again and again until he was positively satiated, and the recurrent déjà vu so sharply foreshadowed what was about to happen that he felt like he was dreaming with his eyes open. Then he'd let time mosey along once again, to see what came next.

In his late thirties, he'd discovered there were limits as to how far back he could go. At the time, he was more or less happily married, with two young children and a routine home life. But one afternoon in town, he'd happened to catch sight of Sally coming out of the post office. He hadn't seen her for years. She was gorgeous. It started him reminiscing. When he got back home, he locked himself in the den and removed the watch from its hiding place in a drawer to which only he had the key. He wanted to relive that afternoon they had spent together. Never mind what came later, the look upon her face, the disdain; never mind her annoyance at his intrusion, as if that particular path in that specific patch of woods near her home by rights belonged to her; never mind the gut-wrenching heartache that turned him inside out the whole day long, until he could get home from school and flee into the future. After all these years, what harm was there in wanting to once again fondle her youthful breasts and lick her pert nipples in the warm cocoon of that sun-drenched, rattan-sofa afternoon… in wanting to return, however ephemerally, to what he now remembered as his most beguiling brush with carnal revelation? Yet to his dumbfounded chagrin, the hour hand had refused to backtrack that far. The past beyond a decade or so had proven irretrievable.

His disconcertion was short-lived. Curious as to why Sally had come back to town in the first place, he had turned the crown the other way and stumbled upon a fresh recollection of the two of them agreeing to meet the next day. Advancing the minute hand just a wee bit more, it suddenly came to him that he and Sally had spent the weekend together. Her nipples were as pointy as ever, and the top button of her pants had been more than happy to yield to his fingers.

'Wait a minute!'

Fiddling with the crown, he edged the minute hand back ever so slightly, till the weekend came into view. From that point on, and for two full years, he left the watch to keep time for itself. He and Sally jumped head over heels from an adulterous lovers' tryst into a whirlwind passion that swept him off his feet — he left his wife and kids, a divorce was pronounced, and life took on an intensity that surpassed anything he had ever experienced. His bliss was replete.

But it didn't last. And what followed made it afterwards far too painful for him to ever envisage reliving their time together, much less anything from his past. Anything he could reach with the watch, that is.

Demoralised by the debacle with Sally, he started turning the crown in search of something better down the road; but though he advanced the watch time and again — though he routinely peeked round the next bend, over the hill, past the corner — he never found the good fortune he sought. Until, one day, indifferent to the consequences, he egged the hands forward on their fateful course.

The hour hand neared midnight.

He guessed what awaited him in the end.

¢³

Death stood before his errand, genuinely surprised.

'So, all this time, it was you who had my watch.'

'It was me. You never knew?'

'I never knew,' said Death. He shook his head and smiled to himself. 'Did you know it was my watch?'

The elderly man in the armchair considered the timepiece in his hand.

'No, I didn't. But I found out what it could do.'

Death raised his brows in query.

'What did you make of it?'

His errand's gaze wandered to the window. Outside, there was a bright midday sun. The afternoon to come would be like the one he and Sally had shared so long ago.

'I don't see the point. Of the watch, I mean.'

Death followed his errand's gaze. He appeared to be considering some trees in the distance. Their leaves were fluttering in the waning breeze.

'Well, I can put it this way: some people have a hard time believing their life has actually come to an end; that, be it day or night, their midnight hour has arrived.'

'I don't mean that. I mean being able to go backwards in time. Or forwards. What's the point?'

'Oh,' said Death. 'I see. Yes, that's a fair question.'

There was a matching armchair. He settled himself into it.

'It's a function that sometimes comes into play. You see, you have choice. You always have choice. How to use your time. What you choose to do. How you treat others. How you treat yourself. Your whole life long, you choose. Few truly realise how much freedom they have, to choose how they live. The watch can take someone back to any point in their past. From that point on, they have the possibility to choose differently.'

His errand pondered this. He had never gone back in time to make a different choice. He had always gone back to relive his moments of good fortune, exactly as they had occurred. He'd been greedy to possess all that had felt good in his life.

'Some of my errands hope to make a few amends before they leave,' continued Death. 'Sometimes they beg for a second chance, a new lease on life… in hopes of doing better.'

All they had to do was ask, thought Death. But when they had their chance, rarely did they ever change anything. Mostly, they'd ignore the tinglings of intuition, the ticklings of déjà vu. Few if any ever woke up. Consequently, they'd miss the same opportunities and make the same mistakes. They would say the same hurtful words, slam the same doors shut, dance the same true-to-character moves. In the end, they'd find they'd tallied up the selfsame bottom line. And once again it was their own fault. The second time he'd find them, they were generally at a loss and ready to move on.

'And being able to go forwards? What's the point of that?'

'That feature comes into play more often. It's what enables a person to finalise their suicide, when that is what they choose.'

The old man gave Death a quizzical look.

'The hands have to read midnight before their time can be up,' explained Death. 'But it's not for me to do; they themselves must advance the hands. All the way. Until the watch shows midnight.'

'Well, it never crossed my mind to take my own life,' countered the old man. 'After all, I had the watch and I knew what it could do. But years ago, I did try to advance the hands once to midnight, just to see. And I found it wasn't possible. It's just like going backwards in time. You can only go so far, and then the hands seize up and won't budge.'

An epiphany brightened Death's brow. He looked outside. A happy thought crossed his mind — *I'll get your goat, You old Goat.*

'There's a safety catch,' said Death matter-of-factly. 'To get past it, you have to turn the bow a quarter turn.'

The elderly man looked at the watch. He took hold of the bow between his fingers.

'Does it matter which way it's turned?'

'Same as with the crown. Clockwise if you want the hands to advance, counterclockwise if you want them to retreat.'

He could see the wheels turning in his errand's mind. It took a little while before a coherent thought formed in the folds of the worn-out grey matter, but the old man suddenly sat up and looked at Death with wide-eyed hope.

'What's stopping me from turning the hands all the way back?'

Death feigned surprise.

'All the way back? Why? You can't do that.'

'Why not?' insisted the old man, brandishing the watch in his fist. 'What's stopping me? Are you going to stop me?'

'Heavens no,' said Death soothingly. He hoped his errand wouldn't drop the watch in his excitement. A broken watch wouldn't do either of them any good.

'Then why can't I?'

'I didn't say you couldn't. You can.'

'You said I couldn't.'

'Did I? But of course you can. It's just that… I can't…'

'You can't what?'

Death hesitated.

'You can't what? You can't allow it? Is that it? Why?'

'Why…'

He left him on tenterhooks. Just to be sure he'd landed him.

'Same as with the suicides,' Death finally answered. 'I can't do it for you.'

The old man started.

'But… I'm not asking you to.'

'Then what's stopping you?'

The silence in the room said it all: nothing. The old man looked at the watch. The three hands were pointing straight up. He was at the threshold. Decisively, he gave the bow a quarter turn, seized the crown with his fingers, and began twirling it counterclockwise. With bated breath, he watched as the hands spun round faster and faster than ever before. Round and round, stela after stela. Further and further, till the future receded into darkness and the distant past appeared in the mists. And as the years sped by, his quest became clear: that moment in time when it all began, in the schoolyard, when Sally had kissed him for the first time. The morning when he had found the watch. It came into view and he was a youth once again and he felt himself at home and it was the morning and he woke up in his room.

‘You cheated.’

Death eyed God equably.

‘You’re annoyed.’

‘You’re damn right I’m annoyed,’ groused God. ‘By what right did you let him go so far back? No one should be able to reverse the course of time that much.’

‘You’re the One who designed the eventuality into the watch in the first place.’

That was true. God glowered.

‘That’s not the point,’ He retorted.

‘It’s not the point because You’re sore I got the watch back. You were happier when You had me in the dark. You were gloating in Your Beard, You old Goat.’

God’s scowl softened. He liked it when Death called him a goat.

‘Besides, he was shaking his fist. I was afraid he might break it. And We wouldn’t want that, now, would We?’

‘Well, so you got the watch back. No worse for wear?’

‘Just wet from the dew.’

‘And the boy? You realise, don’t you, how his life will feel to him now?’

A seraph came in with a well-laden tray. God helped Himself, but Death sat pensively. He did indeed realise how the young boy’s life would feel to him. Now, every truly good moment that came along, every bright stroke of fortune, would feel somewhat hollow, vaguely familiar — and no sooner would it begin than he'd wistfully know it wouldn't last. Whereas life's heartaches and betrayals, defeats and disappointments, mind-numbing ennui and moments of despair, all would overtake him as unchecked unknowns. When they began he'd be filled with fear. How long? How long this time? Every hardship, every tribulation, would be lived to the hilt, blow by blow. To him, life would feel skewed. He would never have the sense that what was good could ever be enough to counterbalance what was bad. It was a sorry fate, and Death felt uneasy. It was he who had lost the watch in the first place.

Noting Death's sombre look, God proffered a goblet.

'Have a sip of nectar, My friend.'

Death looked at the goat.

'What can I do?'

God smiled kindly at His creationary comrade-in-arms.

'What can We ever do, My friend? It's all up to him.'

Death cradled the cup in his hands and stared for a while at the swirling nectar. It looked as if galaxies were doing cartwheels in that chalice.

'Is it enough?' he asked, looking up.

God stared into His friend's beautiful eyes.

'More than enough,' He said. 'And more than that... it's what is.'

The intractable soul

ARCHANGEL ARCHY stared at the shallow brazier that stood to one side near the wall. There was a sharp, rapping knock at the door. His angelic amanuensis looked in.

'Five more minutes,' said Archy, placating her beautiful scowl with pleading eyes. She huffed and shut the door.

His gaze settled back on the brazier. How much more could he take? How many souls need he send on their merry way, before Almighty God would relieve him of this gruelling monotony? It never stopped — fate after fate, soul after soul. When you'd seen a few million, you felt like you'd seen them all; when you'd seen a few *hundred* million, you more or less had. People were the same the world over. The same hopes, the same dreams, the same pains, the same fears. Was it any wonder? They were all cut from the same cloth.

Archy thought back to the day when Yahweh had recruited him eons ago. All of Heaven had been abuzz with the rumour that the great Abba Himself would be emceeing that year's annual festivities in honour of the cherubim. If true, it could mean only one thing: He had singled one out for promotion. And if God were kicking a cherub upstairs, that too, by the law of dominos, could only mean one thing: an empty slot would need to be filled. There'd be a chain-pull reaction down the line. From the lowliest angels to most exalted thrones, every Tom, Dick, and Harry in Heaven was tittering with excitement. Sure enough, Yahweh Himself did run the show, finishing things off with a climax that featured the seraphim choir singing riffs on *Holy, holy, holy* while He duly fastened two additional pairs of wings onto a giddy cherub, turning him into a seraph. There were cheers and hosannas. Everyone felt jubilant.

Afterwards, the great reception hall was overflowing with angelic beings of all stripes mixing and mingling and watching with eagle eyes to see whom God talked to. For His part, Heaven's Head Honcho worked the crowd like a king, smoothing feathers, trading good-natured barbs, calling out across the crowd, and now and then slipping a quiet word to someone while steering them towards the refreshments.

'Archibald! So glad to see you,' said Yahweh, coming up and putting a friendly Arm round His lowly angel's shoulders. He reached out to shake hands all round. 'Harold. Thomas. Richard. Great to see you. Hey, I want you guys to listen up. I've been thinking you should start a barbershop quartet. I'm not kidding. I heard the four of you singing in the lower orbits the other day. Terrific. I mean that. Seriously. Top notch. I want you fellows to play Saint Peter's. I say it's about time we phased out Gregorian and phased in Barberian. Well, looky here — My glass is empty. Can you beat that? Those bacchantic bandits have struck again. Say, Archibald, there's something I've been meaning to ask you… You'll excuse Us, won't you?'

That was how Almighty God had started His pitch, taking him aside for an impromptu face-to-face. Wanted to promote him the to rank of archangel. He was very persuasive.

'Just imagine, Archibald,' God enthused, making it all sound so grand. 'You'll be one of the elite. Your wings will caress thousands of souls. You'll fan their faith. You'll shelter them from despair. There is no finer task under Heaven's dome. I need angels like you. Angels who've proven their mettle. Who are willing to rise in the ranks. Who are willing to put their shoulder to the Great Wheel of Human Strife and keep it turning. What do you say?'

What did he say? Gaga at having been singled out? Chosen by God? His face all aglow? He foolishly said yes. Just like Moses.

'That's my angel!' said Yahweh, beaming with satisfaction. 'Tell you what: We'll upgrade your wings and make it official as soon as We put this shindig to bed. Come on…'

Like a pillar of fire spearheading a holy trek to the Promised Land, God parted the crowd and led His protégé to the drinks table. With His powerful Hand, He snagged an hors-d'œuvre and reached for the bubbly.

'Time to refill My glass. Yours too, before the bacchantes finish this off. Grab yourself one of those tartlets, Archibald — they're delicious. The dominations are tiptop at laying out a spread, I must say.'

Yahweh had raised His flute in a toast.

'Here's to you, Archibald — my newest archangel. And who knows,' He'd added, with a conspiratorial wink, 'in a few eons' time, We'll probably be celebrating your own induction into the seraphim ranks.'

Archy snorted. *A few eons' time.* It already felt like he'd been sitting in this room for an eternity or two. There was no other word for it: he'd been had. An archangel with his duties and position was nothing more than a glorified fate-pusher. Nor was the job grand at all; it consisted of hoodwinking souls on their way back to life — getting them to believe that their hopes had been heard, that their wishes and dreams would find fulfilment in the course of their next incarnation. As if God really cared. That 'Abba' shtick was for show. He was far too removed up there in His Seventh Heaven to concern Himself with piddling little dust bunnies on puny planet Earth. He imagined Himself a Cosmos Creator. A Mass Maker. A Big Bang God with a Universe to run. Yet Archy was expected to pass His Majesty off as a down-to-earth divinity who cared so much about each and every individual being that He even knew how many hairs were on your head.

Well, on Archy's head at least, that count had dwindled to a no-brainer since he'd become an archangel. Zero. Zilch. O for egg. He was now as bald as a coot. Or, as Yahweh had on one occasion hooted, *Archi*-bald.

Archy hadn't taken it kindly. As far as he was concerned, the loss of his once flowing, golden mane was the direct result of the stifling, mind-numbing boredom he'd encountered at higher altitude since moving up the ladder and getting his archangel wings. His scalp had gone flaccid for want of stimulation.

Again, there was a knock at the door and the angel looked in.

'Can we get on with it, Archy? My smile is killing me.'

'Oh, Cynthia, I'm so sorry. Yes, yes, by all means. Please forgive me. Show the next one in. I forget you have to sit there with them.'

'Well, if they're out there, Archy, and you're in here, it's not *you* who's sitting with them — is it.'

'Quite,' he agreed. 'Again, Cynthia: I'm sorry.'

She gave him one of her looks and closed the door. If telepathy were any guide, that particular look relayed a message that went *I'll-let-it-slide-Archy-because-I-know-you're-having-a-hard-time-these-days-but-if-I-ever-find-out-you've-been-wanking-off-in-here-I'll-rip-your-wings-to-shreds-my-dear.*

Cynthia was the best amanuensis in the destiny department and he was lucky to have her. She'd been assigned to him soon after he'd officially changed his name to Archy. Undoubtedly a gift from Yahweh: only "He" could have pried her away from Raguel to team her up with a relative newbie. For what reason? In compensation for the loss of his locks? To make amends for His Archi-bald gibe, now a stock joke in Heaven? Archy didn't care. He'd come to have a clearer picture of God's mysterious ways. They weren't mysterious at all. They were as plain as day to anyone who simply opened his eyes: Almighty God was a high-handed despot.

A despot who had the upper Hand… and who could throw you down on a whim.

'This way, please. This is Archangel Archy. He'll be finalising your return to the world today. Do take a seat.'

Cynthia pointed the soul to a fauteuil that was facing the desk.

'And this, of course, is for you, Archangel Archy.'

Cynthia placed a dossier before him. On the folder, in her neat quillmanship, was the name MILDRED. Turning to go, she glanced over her shoulder and added with a troubled look, *Wait'll-you-see-what-they've-got-in-store-for-her.*

The door was about to close when Archy cleared his throat.

Oh-Cynthia…

She looked back in.

Yes?

You-weren't-serious-about-the-wings-were-you?

Her eyes narrowed.

Just-try-me-you-Archy-winged-wanker-and-we'll-see.

She pulled the door shut in a forceful way that added exclamation to her point.

Archy leaned back uneasily in his chair and considered the soul before him. Mildred.

'Well, Mildred,' he began — 'are you ready to begin?'

'I sure am if you are,' replied the soul with verve. 'I can't wait to get back.'

A trooper. No doubt about it. The sort of soul that can suffer a dozen drubbings ten lifetimes in a row and still believe in the formula *Third time's a charm.* Hardy. Useful. Not good at math.

'Well now, tell me, Mildred: for your life to come, what is your wish?'

'Oh, I don't have one wish,' she chortled. 'I've got a hundred. At least!'

She had the raspy laugh of an inveterate optimist. As a soul, she was definitely getting older, but she was aging better than most. An exception… unlike many others… although, considering the recurrent grind of reincarnation, you could forgive them: after a few hundred lives or so, most souls were worn down to insignificant little flickers. Not that it stopped The Powers That Be from sending them back time and again to serve their purpose in the Grand Scheme of Things, that same dreary mission to grease the cogs. It was a thankless destiny. For his first eon or so, Archy had tried to send off the ill-fated with good cheer. He'd done all he could to nurture their naïve faith that sooner or later their luck would turn… that they'd snag the brass ring, strike the mother lode, get dealt the royal flush. He knew it wouldn't happen — God's Great Plan didn't work that way — but if they went back to Earth bereft of all hope they'd just lie down and die, and the Great Wheel of Human Strife would grind to a stop for want of lubrication.

'A hundred,' he whistled, with ersatz relish. 'Why don't you tell me all about them?'

'Oh, I'm sure I'd bore you to tears,' she answered, grinning good-naturedly. 'You've heard it all before, no? At least once or twice? 'Fess up!'

'Mildred, Mildred,' pooh-poohed Archy obligingly. 'Like snowflakes and stars, no two wishes are alike. Each wish is unique. You can be sure that God in Heaven has heard your every prayer.'

Mildred guffawed.

'If that's so, then I'll bet He's sick of me — in my last life, I gave Him an earful.'

Archy couldn't help but smile. She spoke more truly than she knew.

'Well, Mildred, this is your file. Let's take a look and see what you've been up to in your last life, shall we?'

Archy opened the dossier with a befitting show of solemnity, as if Mildred's past life were something to revere. In fact, and as he knew all too well, it was something to pity. An alcoholic mother; an incestuous father; half a dozen fly-by-night lovers; a saviour who beat her within an inch of her life; two miscarriages; dead-end jobs; unemployment; eviction; homelessness; and finally, release when she froze to death one winter's night on the sidewalk where she'd pitched her bivouac.

'My own fault,' Mildred explained. 'Wasn't forecast, but the wind picked up and changed direction. Being asleep's no excuse. You have to wake up and move to the leeward.'

She was exactly the sort of soul that God liked best: the kind that shouldered all the blame. A poster soul for the *God helps those who help themselves* campaign, who wasn't expecting favours like divine intervention or meteorological moderation. The sort that thanked God for every blessing, however few and far between, while sparing Him incrimination for every affliction, however frequent and profuse. God basked in their adoration and got off scot-free.

'Well, Mildred, I can tell you that God treasures your pluckiness.'

What God really treasured was not being held accountable, thought Archy. He glanced at the fine-print précis of her next life; they'd obviously set her up to continue carrying the cross she'd already borne so willingly too many lifetimes in a row. They clearly had faith in her.

'Plucky and proud of it,' she affirmed. 'I just hope He's got something good in store for me this time round. I ain't complaining, mind you. But if you stick to the rules and keep feeding a one-armed bandit, he's supposed to give you something back for your trouble sooner or later. Know what I mean? Given what I've been through, I should think I'm more than overdue for a jackpot, don't you?'

Mildred laughed as if she were joking, but Archy divined she was clinging to her fallacious logic with wholehearted hope. To steer her away from such thoughts, he fixed her with wide eyes and mock disbelief. Humour was his preferred antidote to the dangers of disenchantment.

'Why, Plucky Mildred. You surprise me. Are you calling God a One-Armed Bandit?'

'Well, if He ain't a One-Armed Bandit, then He sure as hell's a One-Armed Wanker,' giggled Mildred with glee. 'Don't you agree?'

With a glint of mischief in his eye, Archy wagged a finger at her.

'Mildred, Mildred… we mustn't let the Wanker out the bag like that. Not around here. You'll get me into trouble.'

'You? In trouble? Oh, you'd like some trouble, wouldn't you,' she sniggered merrily. 'With that nice Cynthia, I'll bet. She likes you, you know. I saw how she looked at you. Hot as a she-devil, she is. She wants to dig her nails into your wings, that one.'

'Between you and me,' confided Archy archly, 'she thinks I'm a wanker, too.'

While Mildred squealed with mirth, Archy withdrew three sealed envelopes from a pouch inside the folder's front cover and laid them side by side in a neat row on the desk. The first envelope was marked with a yellow "B". The second envelope was marked with a red "S". The third envelope was marked with a blue "D". But otherwise, they were identical.

'Mildred,' resumed Archy with apposite gravitas, 'I am happy to admit that your levity is refreshing, but it is nevertheless Time we got down to Business. I have set here before you three Envelopes. Each Envelope contains a Destiny for your next Incarnation. Every possible effort has been made' — this was standard phrasing, though frankly misleading — 'to ensure that your Destiny will fulfil the Wish you have for your Life to come.'

'Don't forget, I've got a hundred wishes,' interjected Mildred gaily.

Archy ignored her.

'It is Now for you to Choose. For there is No Greater Truth in God's Boundless Creation than this: *You Have Choice.* God does not wish to impose His Will upon you. He leaves it to you to Choose, freely and without constraint. So with that in mind, Mildred, what'll it be — B, S, or D?'

She looked at the three envelopes.

'Why isn't it 1, 2, or 3?'

He met her question with resolute silence.

Mildred carefully considered the three envelopes. Within each one, a Destiny, a Life. A Trajectory of Happenstance and Fortune, Vicissitude and Kismet. She looked up, transfixed by the choice she must make.

'What do you recommend?' she pleaded. 'Do you know what they contain?'

Archy was moved, but unyielding.

'It is for you to choose. Always.'

She hesitated. Apart from her most recent life, her prior incarnations were beyond the reaches of her memory, hidden below the horizon of Time; but although she could recall not even the slightest whisper, she had an amorphous sense that they had been wearying and doleful, yoked to cheerless toil. She wanted a good life for a change. A little happiness each day. Some love that lasted. Was that too much to hope for?

Three envelopes. What if only one was good? What if one was bad, and the other just so-so? Three choices. B, S, or D. Mildred's gaze settled on the middle envelope. Maybe that was the middle of the road, she thought. So-So would be better than bad. Since you couldn't say if good came first, or last — if B were for Bad, or Blessed… if D might mean Delight, or Disaster — choosing B or D could hit you with a total loss just as easily as a jackpot. Maybe it would be safer to lower her sights. Fifty wishes answered were better than none.

'S,' she mumbled. 'S. I choose S.'

Archy rose from his chair. With ceremonial pomp, he collected the B and D envelopes and went to place them in the shallow brazier; they spontaneously combusted and went up in smoke. A sweet, medieval fragrance wafted through the room. Mildred was duly impressed.

'I guess there's no going back?'

'Don't give it a second thought,' said Archy breezily, returning to the desk. He picked up the S envelope and handed it to her. 'You have made your choice, Mildred. Congratulations. A new life awaits you. Please take your envelope to Cynthia. She will see to it that you are woven into the Grand Scheme of Things post-haste.'

Mildred stood up, wobbly on her feet and somewhat let down.

'Wow, that was sure quick. Are my wishes going to be fulfilled?'

Archy had no wish to foster false hopes with fairy tales or fine-sounding words. Mildred's greatest source of strength for getting through her next life would be her own ignorance, pure and simple. He replied as tactfully as he could.

'You will see.'

'Well, thank you so much,' she said politely. 'It's been fun chatting with you.'

Archy nodded.

Mildred looked back when she reached the door.

'You ought to ask that Cynthia out. She's sweet on you.'

Archy said nothing. Walking over to the brazier, he held out his hands above the still warm ashes. He hardly noticed as Mildred went out and closed the door. His mind was elsewhere. He was thinking. To succumb to an errant thought was all it took to become a fallen angel. Once He'd admitted you to Heaven, Yahweh was merciless toward those who might yield to temptation; any angel who failed to toe Heaven's line was sure to be summarily cast down with a one-way ticket straight back to Earth — and for good, with no possibility of redemption. A permanent perforation on the rolls of reincarnation. An odd angel out for all eternity, never to return to the heavenly fold. The utter finality of such an end was terrifying to Archy. It was a fate he would wish on no angel.

Especially an angel he loved.

✌

'He has to sign for this one,' said the power. 'In person.'

Cynthia was staring at the soul they had brought. He was blindfolded, and his wrists were tightly bound with a rope that served as a lead.

'We've never been entrusted with a soul in this manner. Is Archangel Raguel aware of this?'

The power looked at her pointedly.

'He is being entrusted to an archangel, not to you — and it is not for you to ask questions.'

Cynthia stood her ground nonetheless and waited for an answer. It was the power who was holding the rope who relented; when he spoke, his voice rumbled with menace.

'Archangel Raguel is perfectly aware of this… and much else besides.'

Displeased by his tone, Cynthia had a mind to stare him down but thought better of it.

'I see,' she said coolly. 'Please wait one moment.'

With sedate deliberation, she walked down the hall and knocked on Archy's door.

❦

ADAMO.

Archy pondered the name on the folder. He recognised Archangel Samael's authoritative quill. A chill spread through his wings.

The powers had taken him aside and warned him that the soul was intractable. Once they had left — and he was glad to see them go — he'd called Cynthia in and asked her to remove the blindfold while he held the rope, just in case. Not that the soul seemed dangerous in any way. At Cynthia's urging, he had gratefully settled himself in the fauteuil.

Archy gave Cynthia a searching glance as he took the precaution of tying the rope to the desk.

Why-do-you-suppose-they-sent-him-to-me?

She shrugged her shoulders. Even under her robes, he could tell they were strong and shapely.

Do-you-want-me-to-stay?

Archy closed his eyes and willed a thought away. Unseen by either of them, the soul almost smiled.

'Thank you, Cynthia. That will be all,' said Archy. 'I'll call you when I need you.'

Disappointed, she turned and left the room.

Archy watched her go and waited until he heard the door shut. Then he looked back at the soul and was surprised to see him sitting there with a broad smile on his face.

'She's callipygian, too,' said the soul.

'Yes, I know,' said Archy, nodding towards the folder as he took his seat, 'but that isn't her quillwork. It was calligraphed by Archangel Samael, if I'm not mistaken… Adamo.'

'You're not. At least in that regard.'

Archy raised his brows.

'Oh? Did you meet with Archangel Samael?'

'More than once,' replied Adamo calmly.

More than once? Only the most wilful, recalcitrant, indomitable souls were referred to Samael. To have met with him more than once was damning.

'I see. Well, well.'

Though taken aback, Archy was suddenly puzzled.

'What have you been up to?'

Adamo looked at his archangel interlocutor with innocent eyes.

Archy leaned forward. The dossier before him was thicker than any he'd seen cross his desk before, and the cover was worn. This Adamo character was clearly an old soul, but one with more lifetimes to his credit than anyone should have to suffer through to make it to Heaven. He'd obviously been passed over time and again. If that were so, it was for a reason. Archy opened the dossier, expecting the worst. But the worst was not what he expected. The pages it contained were blank.

He flipped through the first few folios and found nothing. Then he hastily riffled the whole dossier, hoping to locate at least one of Adamo's past lives. Every single page was bare. Yet not as a virginal page would be: these were pages that had been fingered and filed time and again; if they were blank, it was because their content had been expunged at some point. Rubbed out. Obliterated. He looked up.

'Nothing, it would seem. How is that?'

Adamo shrugged his shoulders as Cynthia had done.

Archy opened the pouch and withdrew the three envelopes. To his great surprise, they too were blank. And then he understood: this was a soul with more anarchy in him than even the highest archangels had been able to tame. Why they'd sent him down to his level was beyond him, but a blank dossier signified that this Adamo soul was a troublemaker par excellence, with ideas that could corrupt even Heaven itself. Archy decided then and there to wrap things up without delay. He made a conscious effort to steady his voice as he laid the envelopes on the desk.

'Adamo, I think you know why you have been brought to me, and it is Time we got down to Business. I am setting here before you three Envelopes. Each Envelope contains a Destiny for your next Incarnation. Every possible effort has been made to ensure that your Destiny will fulfil the Wish you have for your Life to come. It is Now for you to Choose. For there is No Greater Truth in God's Boundless Creation than this: *You Have Choice.* God does not wish to impose His Will upon you. He leaves it to you to Choose, freely and without constraint…'

'*So with that in mind, Adamo,*' said Adamo, '*what'll it be — B, S, or D?*'

Archy gaped at him.

'Oh, I'm sorry,' said Adamo, leaning forward to inspect the envelopes. 'I see they forgot to mark them. No *Born, Suffer, Die*? I wonder why. Rather odd, wouldn't you agree? Samael's henchangels aren't known to be sloppy. Maybe it was intentional. What do you think?'

Archy was speechless.

'Not that it makes a wit of difference, of course,' Adamo went on, 'since the fate they dictate is the same one in each. But you know that… don't you.'

Of course Archy knew that — he was an archangel — but how did Adamo know? And how in Heaven's name could he possibly remember the B-S-D shorthand? Normally, everything that happened to souls in the celestial realms prior to a return to life was systematically cleared from their explicit memory with each new incarnation, a happy by-product of the ionic dance in the liquor amnii.

'I've been here before,' confided Adamo with an impish grin. 'Don't be surprised.'

'What is this masquerade?' blurted Archy. 'Who the devil are you?'

Adamo's expression turned suddenly thoughtful.

'Confound it, I'm serious,' snapped Archy. 'Who the devil are you! What does this mean, a folder full of blank lives? Everything erased? How do you know about the envelopes, and what they contain?'

It made no sense, but it suddenly crossed Archy's mind.

'Are you a fallen angel?'

A disarming smile spread across Adamo's face. His eyes twinkled.

'I am not a fallen angel. I have never been an angel, nor have ever wished to be. So I cannot be a fallen angel. I am a soul, as you once were, and… perhaps still are, in your heart of hearts?'

Adamo's words hit home with soul-wrenching force. Archy sank back in his chair. In the twinkling of Adamo's eye, the house of cards that until that instant had supported Archy's entire faith came crashing down with a din akin to down feathers settling after a pillow fight.

'Who are you?' whispered Archy, his voice unsteady.

'Just a soul, like you. A freewheeling being. A little bit here, a little bit there… a little bit everywhere. A galaxy unto myself in this swirling mystery of Life.'

'Are you the devil? Are you Satan?'

'The devil? You surprise me… and surely you know who Satan is.'

'Please. Don't say another word,' breathed Archy. 'You've said too much already.'

The room was as steady as a rock. It was Archy's head that was spinning. He was sure the powers would come barging in at any moment to seize him forthwith. The maelstrom in his mind raged on for several long minutes as Adamo observed him with compassionate amusement, patiently waiting for his discomfort to abate. Still the door was not thrown open. No powers came storming in. Even Cynthia didn't knock. Nothing materialised to disrupt the peace that seemed so strangely precarious.

Archy reconsidered things. He needn't compromise himself. All angels had occasional doubts. All were prone to the passing errant thought. It was what you did with such thoughts that mattered. Did you act on them, or leave them unsaid, undone? It was what you did that mattered. And so far, he hadn't done anything. All he need do was send this agent provocateur on his way and be done with him. That was no doubt why they'd sent him along in the first place, just to get rid of him.

Composing himself, Archy straightened up and cleared his throat.

'It remains for you to choose one of the three envelopes, Adamo. That is why you are here. And I am here to witness your choice. So please: choose.'

Adamo lifted up his bound wrists.

'With my hands tied?'

'Yes, with your hands…'

Archy's voice trailed off. Being bound did seem hardly compatible with the notion of choosing freely and without constraint. He stood up and went round the desk; but then he stopped in his tracks. He had no idea what this Adamo devil was capable of. His hands were tied for a reason.

'Allow me to assist you,' Archy countered. 'Which one do

you want? This one? Or this one?'

Adamo grinned and shook his head.

'Ah,' said Archy, picking up the third envelope. 'This one?'

Adamo shook his head again.

'Then which one?'

'None of them. None of the three will do for me.'

'But… but you have to choose, Adamo.'

'I just did.'

There were sounds of commotion down the hall.

'Adamo, listen to me. You can't choose not to choose. You have to choose one of the three,' pressed Archy.

'If I Have Choice, as you say — and I do,' said Adamo — 'and if, as we know to be true, the three envelopes contain the self-same destiny — then the Choice I so inalienably have can only be found in my being free *not* to choose. Should I so wish. Which I do. That is my choice.'

The door was thrown open. The powers had returned.

☙

Archy fluttered about near the ceiling. He'd gone to inspect the cobwebs in the upper reaches of the cell. That there were cobwebs at all surprised him.

'Why in the world are there cobwebs? This is Heaven, not Earth. There aren't any spiders in Heaven.'

'True. There are no spiders in Heaven,' confirmed Adamo from below. 'At least, I've never seen one. But cobwebs give the place such a nice prison touch. Don't you think?'

Cynthia was sitting across from him, on a hard pew that ran the length of the wall.

'Familiar with prison, are we?'

Adamo considered her with sympathy as he massaged his sore wrists. He was glad they'd removed the rope.

'You angels so rarely see the dark side of the moon… or the underbelly of God.'

'Whereas *you*, Adamo — a thorn in His side — have clearly been making the rounds for eons,' said Archy, descending from his tour of inspection.

'Well, yes and no,' said Adamo. 'I've never been this far, actually. It's quite thrilling.'

'Listen to him. *Thrilling.* I should be so happy.'

Cynthia cocked her head to one side. She could just make out the fluttering of wings.

'Someone's coming.'

'Oh goody,' said Adamo cheerfully. 'That means we're going to be hauled before the bench.'

'The throne,' corrected Archy.

'Oh, is that what He sits on? I wonder how many scrolls He goes through, getting a load off His mind.'

Archy and Cynthia hardly had time to catch Adamo's drift much less visualise his thought when half a dozen powers appeared to escort the three of them to the Hall of Judgement. Almighty God was already there, comfortably installed in suitable glory on an elevated throne that was illuminated by a flood of brilliant white light and held aloft by four wheely thrones. With an unflinchingly unforgiving gaze, Yahweh looked sternly down as the powers led Adamo to the dock that stood centre stage at the edge of the circle of light. Archy and Cynthia were ushered to separate positions on either side, in the penumbra just beyond. As their eyes adjusted, they perceived in the darkness of the hall an untold number of angelic spectators hailing from the three spheres, discreetly fanning themselves and each other in their excitement.

A cohort of clerical thrones materialised in a half circle before the accused to chant the charges being brought by God against Adamo. Replete with gripes of every stripe, the long-winded recital, Archy soon realised, concerned every single life Adamo had ever lived on Earth. This was no ordinary trial. This was a Showdown, a Face-Off, a Grand Finale — prepared in advance with painstaking thoroughness and with one and only one outcome in mind. No wonder all the lives in the dossier had been erased: their entire contents had been expunged to ensure that nothing whatsoever could conceivably be produced as evidence in defence of the accused. When they'd sent him to Archy, The Powers That Be had been giving Adamo one last chance to capitulate and defer to God's Lordship, to return to Earth and abide by His Rules. But he had refused to be cowed, refused to consent to a mockery of his free will. The time had come to settle things once and for all.

For Adamo, listening to the litany of charges was like taking a stroll down memory lane. He'd lost track of how many shenanigans he'd pulled, how many times he'd fomented rebellion, how anarchistically he'd agitated in favour of freedom. He found it all hugely amusing, and he couldn't stop smiling.

His boyish grin and stifled snickers, however, proved disconcerting to the chanting thrones. Mustering the tenacity of papal bulldogs, they fought like the dickens to see their spiel through without missing a beat. Their struggle was epic. Some three hours later, unanimously relieved to have finally reached the score's bold double bar, the thrones chanted the very last charge and shouted a resounding *'Amen!'*

Their relief was shared by the assembly as a whole. Applause broke out, and a recess was called.

The spectators adjourned to stretch their wings and investigate the refreshments buffet. The defendants, barred from the festivities, were escorted back to their cell.

❧

'I had no idea it was you,' said Cynthia.

Filled with admiration and a smidgen star-struck, she'd been realising that, prior to becoming an angel, she had often had a fondness for the very people Adamo had once been. Though she'd never met him personally in any of her incarnations, his examples and teachings in all their many forms — long since recorded in books and scriptures, stories and songs — had often inspired her. Those long-ago memories came back to her now, and she was tingling with excitement.

'You can't say I was wrong, when I asked if you were the devil,' added Archy. 'You've been plenty tarred and feathered with that epithet.'

Adamo laughed.

'I wouldn't have it any other way. But why are people so un-true to their hearts? Why don't they stand up for their souls, judge for themselves? Why do they abdicate their lives? Why do they kneel and grovel and prostrate themselves? Why do they love their chains? Their slavery? I've never understood.'

Cynthia rebuked him with a sceptical wink.

'I don't believe you.'

'All right,' he conceded, blushing a little. 'It's not that I've never understood. It's just that I've never wished to acquiesce to this fear of being, this fear of freedom… for surely there is nothing more precious than being *free* to *be*. After all, the true fun in life is found in freely exploring and discovering who *you* are, as you improvise a tune like no other. Being who you are, unique in all the universe — that is Life, its very essence.

'But if you're afraid to be yourself, if you're afraid to be free, to be on your own, then doubt overwhelms you. *Tell me who I am! Tell me what to do! Don't leave me alone!* Into a breach like that steps a tyrant who says, Follow Me! How thankful you are. Answers? *At last! Hallelujah!* Truth? *Yes! The Tyrant's Truth!* Your Saviour? *Glory be! The Shepherd Himself!* You make him your god. You put your faith in him. And the more you adore him — grateful for His Words, His Laws, His Sermons and Scriptures — the more blinkered and biddable you become. The more subservient you grow to be, the more he exalts you. He'll even take you up to Heaven. Pin wings on you. Make you an angel. Those who rise to the highest angelic orders are the souls with the least will of their own. Yes-souls par excellence. Come to think of it, I think they've abandoned their souls altogether. Those throne thrones, you know, they've definitely got a screw loose, the way they wheel about. And look at the seraphim. They're down to one word.'

'Adamo, for Heaven's sake,' said Archy earnestly. 'Stop making light of all this. Don't you realise what you're risking here?'

'The truth is light, Archy. And I don't know what you mean. I'm not risking anything.'

Archy's eyes widened.

'Whatever do you mean? Of course you're risking something. And not just being cast down like some fallen angel. You're staking your soul here, Adamo. Your very soul!'

Amplified by a shaky conviction, Archy's voice filled the cell with tremulous exasperation. His fears and doubts rebounded off the walls.

'Don't you understand? This is your Last Judgement. This is the end of the road to Heaven for you. You either fall to your knees now and pray for Mercy, or He'll cast you down to Hell for all time. You'll be eternally damned. Or… God forbid! — even worse: He'll annihilate your soul.'

Hearing this, Adamo stood up. With a few measured steps, he came over to where Archy was seated and crouched down. Gazing into his eyes, he spoke calmly.

'Surely you know this by now, Archy. The soul is not mortal. It is Eternal. Unchanging. Indivisible. It is One with God. It *is* God. It has always been and will always Be. It cannot be annihilated. You needn't worry. You are God. As am I. As is Cynthia.'

'That's blasphemy,' squeaked Archy, suddenly quite pale. 'Isn't it?'

'Don't be obtuse, Archy,' said Cynthia. 'You know he's right.'

'We are each of us God. So too is the One who sits in that hall. But he has raised himself up and become an Accuser. It is he who is Satan. He's a tyrant. He has gathered about himself a multitude of docile sheep who bleat and pray and appeal to him, who submit to his will, who live in fear of his anger and wrath and judgement. But it is they who give him power over their lives — were it not for their consent, he would have none whatsoever. It is they themselves who bring anger and wrath and judgement upon their heads. They themselves. He just takes credit for it.'

Adamo patted Archy's knee.

'We're free, Archy. Always free. Free to dance to the music of our souls. You don't have to dance to his tune.'

⁂

The proceedings reconvened. From his designated spot in the penumbra, Archy eyed Cynthia. She was standing tall and straight, and she looked more lovely than ever. He could see by her bearing that Adamo's words had borne fruit. She had chosen her camp: she knew what she wanted. She would be a fallen angel before the end of the trial.

Archy mused that when they were done with Adamo, the thrones of God would be calling on him, to make clear his position. *A vacillation has been detected in your conduct,* they would chant, *one that suggests a less-than-ardent belief in the Righteousness of God and His Heaven. Concerns have been raised that temptation may have compromised your integrity. Errant thoughts have been surmised. You must answer before God, not only for your words and deeds, but above all for your soul: Are you with Him? Wholeheartedly? With undivided loyalty and unwavering devotion? Or not? What say you, Archangel Archibald, aka 'Archy'?*

Archy stood there trying to feel his love for God. It was no use. His devotion had already waned, eons ago. It was what he felt for Cynthia that now filled his heart.

The clerical thrones were calling for objections.

'Hear ye! Hear ye! Are there any objections to the charges? Quibbles? Cavils? Does anyone wish to raise his voice in defence of the accused? Speak now, or be very, very still!'

No wing stirred. The celestial assembly was mute with one voice.

'The assembly has spoken! You may resume fanning yourselves. We will now hear from the accused. What have you to say for yourself, Adamo? How do you answer these damning charges? How do you plead before Almighty God: Guilty, or Not Guilty?'

Adamo was matter-of-fact.

'I plead nothing at all.'

The thrones received this bombshell with an awkward silence. Only after a very long moment did one of them finally manage a timorous, 'Nothing at all?'

Adamo shook his head.

'Nope. Nothing at all.'

Drumming His Fingers on the arm of His throne, Almighty God glowered. This damnable Adamo was forcing His Hand.

'Answer the question!' He fulminated. 'How do you plead before Me: Guilty or Not Guilty?'

Adamo looked up and winked.

'Souls that are enslaved plead. Not me. I'm free.'

A hushed apprehension gripped the hall. With prescient dread, everyone present knew what was coming. Were it not for their browbeaten sense of decorum, angels and archangels, principalities and powers, virtues and dominations, thrones and cherubim and even the seraphim would have been springing from their seats and storming the exits in a free-for-all flight before the floodgates burst and all hell broke loose. Nevertheless, duty — and no small measure of morbid curiosity as to whether the refreshments buffet would survive the deluge — kept them riveted to their seats.

'What did you say?' smouldered Yahweh, staring down imperiously at Adamo.

Adamo replied with cordial frankness.

'I said, *Souls that are enslaved—*'

'I know what you said!' barked God, suddenly enraged. 'I'm God, confound it! I know everything!'

'That's not true at all,' said Adamo. 'You don't know what I'm thinking.'

As the straw that broke the camel's back, as the drop that made the cup runneth over, as the spark that blew the powder keg sky high, so this forthrightly stated and manifestly incontestable fact unleashed a celestial cataclysm. Almighty God blew His stack. Quadrupling the portion with which He'd lambasted Job, Yahweh brought a torrential, sixteen chapter harangue crashing down upon Adamo's head, determined to demolish every last trace of His nemesis' fearless refusal to knuckle under and submit to His Divine Will. With unmuffered fury, He raged and stormed, huffed and puffed, and blew the top off the celestial dome. Sure enough, to everyone's chagrin (but to no one's surprise), the refreshments buffet was wiped out by a particularly virulent gust of holy pique.

At last, His Face royally flushed with righteous indignation, God recapped His diatribe, putting His overarching vaunt into a nutshell.

'Nothing in Heaven or on Earth is like Me, One without fear!' He roared. 'No purpose of Mine can be thwarted! I can do all things!'

Drawing Himself up, Almighty God thundered His Final Last Word with full-blown scriptural emphasis.

'I AM! I AM WHAT I AM!'

His pealing Words reverberated and rumbled and bounced off the walls for what seemed like an eon until silence at last timidly reasserted itself.

God waited. All eyes were on the accused.

With the innocence of a child, Adamo smiled.

'I AM, too.'

There was a stunned silence.

Looking down from His throne, Yahweh smugly anticipated that pandemonium would erupt any second: His celestial slaves weren't going to let an affront like that go by without howling in protest and swarming to tear Adamo limb from limb. But the seconds ticked by and no one moved.

Adamo turned and stepped down from the dock. Taking the centre aisle, he walked up the length of the hall row by row and disappeared into the darkness at the very end. A door was heard to open and shut.

Cynthia looked over at Archy.

I'm-leaving-too, came her thought. *How-about-you?*

I'd-say-it's-now-or-never…

Cynthia led the way and Archy followed her up the aisle. On either side, innumerable angels and archangels, principalities and powers, virtues and dominations, thrones and cherubim and even seraphim watched as they passed. In their eyes, one could see they had doubt in their hearts.

Meanwhile, squirming with Self-consciousness, God was feeling like a Fool. Suddenly, He sensed His throne being lowered. The four wheely thrones set the imposing chair on the stage and without so much as a by-Your-leave, rolled themselves away up the aisle. They were the first to go. Then, without a word, without a murmur, every angelic being there present followed in turn.

They left Almighty God to turn out the white light by Himself.

☙

It was many eons and incarnations later that Archy and Cynthia and Adamo and Yahweh all found themselves together one day, sitting under a trellised grape vine shading the tables lined up along the terrace of a small kafeneio in a sleepy village by the sea. They were playing cards and drinking retsina to pass the time. Cynthia was leading going into the third round; Adamo was taking a beating. Yahweh looked relaxed, as if he had a card up his sleeve in case of need.

'Could you bring us another round, please,' said Archy to the owner as she passed by.

'Let's make it a bottle,' called Yahweh after her. 'Oh! And more tartlets, too! You know, they're nearly as tasty as the ones the dominations used to make for Me.'

Cynthia frowned.

'Stop capitalising your pronouns. Haven't you gotten over that yet? It's a bad habit. For God's sake, Adamo — play already, will you?'

Adamo had no choice but to lay down his 3.

'Ha!' crowed Yahweh, producing a 9. 'Bastra!'

He scooped up five cards and added them to his pile.

This neatly turned the tables on Cynthia's lead. The play went quickly after that, and by the time the wine and tartlets arrived, Yahweh had taken the game. The owner filled their glasses and left the bottle on the table.

'As you can see, my friends, I'm still mighty Mighty.'

'And just as keen, I see, to Lord it over us when you're favoured by fortune,' teased Adamo, passing him the group's laurel wreath.

'What can I say, Adamo? Fortune raises up a new god every day,' declared Yahweh with satisfaction, placing the laurels on his head. 'Today she crowned me. Tomorrow, if she likes you better than Cynthia or Archy, maybe you'll get the crown.'

'To our kafeneio's elohim,' said Archy, raising his glass.

'Yiamas, yiamas…'

They toasted each other and clinked their glasses and sat for a while, savouring the balmy afternoon and the tartlets and the wine. The terrace overlooked the sea. In the distance they could see one of the village's fishing boats heading back to port. The sky was blue, and a warm breeze was herding a flock of puffy white clouds across the bay.

'Tell me something,' said Cynthia. 'Since that day so long ago when you came down from that silly throne of yours, have you ever thought of hoisting yourself back up there again?'

'Never,' replied Yahweh, his mouth full. Crumbs of tartlet tumbled down his beard. Archy passed him a napkin.

'And why not?' Adamo wanted to know. 'Don't you sometimes miss Heaven?'

'No. I sometimes miss the dominations' cooking,' he said, flicking crumbs from his beard, 'but I don't miss Heaven. Paradise is here, on Earth.'

'But the power, Yahweh — the power. Surely you miss that,'

suggested Archy. 'All those devout souls, trembling on their knees, fearing your wrath, craving your grace, praying to You and only You for salvation?'

'Don't start with the pronouns. Cynthia's right about that. And no, I don't miss that, either. Too many prayers to ward off all the livelong day. Worse than flies.'

Cynthia helped herself to another tartlet.

'Well, what about all those fine-feathered lackeys you had, fanning your brow and singing your praises? The seraphim were your biggest fans.'

Yahweh rolled his eyes.

'Don't remind me. Over and over and over. *Holy, holy, holy.* There was no way to shut them up. But when you pompously park your butt on Heaven's throne, as I foolishly did, being sur-rounded by a birdbrained chorus is par for the course. Keeps your soul well washed, ripe for delusion. No wonder. Hearing yourself loopily praised is guaranteed to addle the spirit. I'm proof of that.'

The grape leaves above their heads rustled, as if to concur.

Yahweh took a meditative sip of wine and contemplated the distant horizon with a faraway look in his eyes.

'No, my friends. I can tell you that there are far better things in life than to be worshipped as the All-Mighty, All-Powerful, All-Knowing Lord of Creation and King of the Heap. Let some other blowhard lay claim to a patch of God-turf if he feels the need. I'm happy to sit back and thumb my nose at the fraudster while he tyrannizes the world into singing his praises and stok-ing his glory. Me, I've learned better.'

Yahweh reached for the bottle and topped up their glasses. He raised his own in a toast.

'Here's to us, my friends! And to the Truth even I came to know —'

His eyes twinkled playfully.

'A happy soul is a free soul… and a free soul is God being happy.'

A·B·C· EDITIONS
17840 • LA BRÉE • FRANCE
ABCEDITIONS.COM

REMERCIEMENTS À
F.F. • R.C.

IMPRIMÉ AU ROYAUME-UNI,
AUX ÉTATS-UNIS, ET DANS D'AUTRES PAYS

THE PIG WHO WISHED TO BE A HORSE … AND OTHER TALES
©2017, 2026 BY PETER GILLIES • ISBN 978-2-9546352-6-2
PRIX PUBLIC EN FRANCE LORS DE LA PARUTION • 14,95
DÉPÔT LÉGAL • JUIN 2017